Growin[g up, she'd dreamed of having] kids on[e day, imagining the perfect] moment when she would tell her husband the happy news.

Telling the father of her child for real was not turning out remotely like her fantasies.

Pulse pounding, she waited for him to say something. Anything.

Gil simply stared at her, unblinking, his face devoid of expression, schooled in a way that revealed nothing. But even that relayed far too much. If he'd been happy, that would have overflowed. There would have been no reason to hide emotion from her.

Disappointment squeezed her heart, for herself and for her child. But for that baby's sake, Neve stayed on the porch with her teeth chattering from the cold rather than run into her cabin and slam the door in his face. No matter how things went between them, she needed to maintain communication lines.

Gil cleared his throat, tipping his head to the side. "Could you repeat that, please? I'm not certain I heard you correctly."

Anger crackled inside her. She was pretty sure her diction had been crystal clear. All the same, she said—again, "I'm pregnant. The baby is yours."

Dear Reader,

What a delight to celebrate my tenth Top Dog Dude Ranch novel with a Christmas story! While the book can be read as a stand-alone, the holiday setting presented the perfect scenario for appearances by characters from earlier books in the series. In particular, *Their Festive Forever* shares more about the heroine's sisters, Isobel (*A Fairy-Tail Ending*) and Zelda (*Charming the Cowboy*). I had a blast crafting their all-inclusive Christmas celebration full of family and community where no one has to cook, clean or do the dishes!

Thank you for picking up a copy of *Their Festive Forever*. I appreciate your support for my stories! Check out my website (catherinemann.com) for monthly contests/giveaways, appearances, upcoming releases, social media links and the sign-up form for my newsletter. I've also recently added information for book clubs/libraries interested in scheduling a Zoom chat with me at one of your meetings.

Wishing you a joyous holiday season full of family, friends, love and, of course, books!

Happy Holidays,

Cathy

THEIR FESTIVE FOREVER

CATHERINE MANN

Harlequin
SPECIAL EDITION

If you purchased this book without a cover you should be aware that this book is stolen property. It was reported as "unsold and destroyed" to the publisher, and neither the author nor the publisher has received any payment for this "stripped book."

MIX
Paper | Supporting responsible forestry
FSC® C021394
www.fsc.org

Harlequin
SPECIAL EDITION™

Recycling programs for this product may not exist in your area.

ISBN-13: 978-1-335-18017-9

Their Festive Forever

Copyright © 2025 by Catherine Mann

All rights reserved. No part of this book may be used or reproduced in any manner whatsoever without written permission.

Without limiting the author's and publisher's exclusive rights, any unauthorized use of this publication to train generative artificial intelligence (AI) technologies is expressly prohibited.

This is a work of fiction. Names, characters, places and incidents are either the product of the author's imagination or are used fictitiously. Any resemblance to actual persons, living or dead, businesses, companies, events or locales is entirely coincidental.

For questions and comments about the quality of this book, please contact us at CustomerService@Harlequin.com.

TM and ® are trademarks of Harlequin Enterprises ULC.

Harlequin Enterprises ULC
22 Adelaide St. West, 41st Floor
Toronto, Ontario M5H 4E3, Canada
www.Harlequin.com

HarperCollins Publishers
Macken House, 39/40 Mayor Street Upper,
Dublin 1, D01 C9W8, Ireland
www.HarperCollins.com

Printed in Lithuania

USA TODAY bestselling author **Catherine Mann** is the author of over a hundred contemporary romance titles, released in more than twenty countries. Catherine's novels have won numerous awards, including a RITA® Award, the *RT Book Reviews* Reviewers' Choice Award and the Booksellers' Best Award. After years of moving around the country, Catherine has settled back in her home state of South Carolina with her Harley-riding husband. Empty nesters, they have a blended family of nine children, nine grandchildren, two dogs and three feral cats. FMI, visit her website: catherinemann.com.

Books by Catherine Mann

Harlequin Special Edition

Top Dog Dude Ranch

Their Festive Forever
Charming the Cowboy
A Fairy-Tail Ending
Last-Chance Marriage Rescue
The Cowboy's Christmas Retreat
Last Chance on Moonlight Ridge
The Little Matchmaker
The Cowgirl and the Country M.D.
The Lawman's Surprise

Montana Mavericks: The Tenacity Social Club

A Maverick's Road Home

Montana Mavericks: The Anniversary Gift

Maverick's Secret Daughter

Visit the Author Profile page
at Harlequin.com for more titles.

To my grandchildren. Your smiles, giggles and hugs are the very best Christmas gift of all!

Chapter One

Neve Dalton usually loved snowy December days with the pristine blanket of white coating the land, thin, but fresh and new. The crisp nip in the air. The taste of snowflakes on her tongue as she indulged in a quiet walk through the woods to spot evening grosbeaks in the spruce firs.

But not today.

Instead, she was freezing her butt off watching a raucous snow-polo match. Neve hugged her arms closer around herself to preserve body heat, even though she wore a parka, gloves, and knit cap. Her toes were turning to ice cubes inside her lined boots as she stood on the sidelines.

The Top Dog Dude Ranch in Tennessee had provided the perfect location to work on her textbook about preserving wildlife even in a recreational setting. As a bonus, she'd had endless opportunities to recharge with a variety of activities, from outdoor adventures to indoor crafts. Even game nights, hoedowns, and live entertainment. Who wouldn't love to stay in a vacation destination where both of her sisters lived? But her six-month stay was rapidly coming to a close.

Boisterous shouts filled the air as the home team, made up of Top Dog staff, scored a goal. Was it called a *goal* in polo? She wasn't sure.

Still, she needed to stick it out to the end of the game—the match?—even though she wasn't cheering on a boyfriend or a relative. In fact, the broad-shouldered subject of her undivided attention no longer held her affection. He was an ex. A fling.

And in about six months, Gil Hadley would be the father of her baby. A little detail she couldn't delay telling him for much longer. She hadn't even told her two sisters, who were currently standing on either side of her. Thank heaven for winter clothing that allowed her to hide the gentle swell of her stomach. Although she wasn't sure how much longer she would be able to hide the morning sickness.

She was determined to share the news about the baby with Gil after the match.

Neve stuffed her fists into the pockets of her puffy jacket, shifting from one freezing foot to the other until the bells on her boots jingled. Was she fidgeting from nerves? Or attraction? Both, most likely.

Horses galloped across the field, hooves thundering as the crimson ball glided over the frozen earth. Gil's athleticism couldn't be denied. His exuberance, too, with his unrestrained laugh carrying over the melee. A tingle of excitement, and perhaps even a bit of envy, rippled through her.

As the last picked in gym class all the way through high school, Neve stifled a twinge of insecurity. She was just fine being the nerdy girl and definitely happy with her professional success as a professor. Her sabbatical these past months to finish writing a textbook had been a surprise, the type of honor she hadn't dared hope for back when she was getting hit in the head during dodgeball.

The cautionary memory had her retreating a step away from the polo field. Just to be on the safe side for the baby's sake. She'd taken up tennis in the years since high school, and her hand-eye coordination had improved accordingly, but she still wouldn't trust her reaction time if that red ball sailed her way.

Staff from the Top Dog Dude Ranch wore blue jackets, playing a team of guests in red. The hobbyist group had booked a retreat and requested a match. The sure-footed horses tossed their heads and danced with excitement, their manes rippling.

From the enthusiastic crowd response, this would no doubt become a frequent offering. A handful were even livestreaming the action.

She'd never heard of snow polo before, much less seen a match. Since Gil had been hired to oversee outdoor sports, all sorts of new adventures had been added to the Top Dog Dude Ranch offerings. Ziplining. Whitewater rafting. Rappelling.

No question, the man had a taste for pushing boundaries.

And he looked mighty fine in the process.

Beside her, Neve's sisters clapped and cheered. Zelda's fella played on the team, and Isobel's guy tended the extra horses on hand in case any on the field grew tired or stressed.

"Whoo-hoo," her sister Zelda shouted, fist pumping the air. Zelda was the rebel of the trio, quirky in her clothes and zest for life. She worked as a dog groomer at the ranch, caring for guest pets as well as the animals in residence. Zelda whooped it up, cradling her small Maltese mix in her arms.

"Good try," Isobel affirmed. Isobel was the wholesome one, an earth-mother type who made her living as a blogger, the writings told from the viewpoint of her daughter's service dog, Cocoa. Little Lottie had been born with spina bifida and used the working animal for mobility assistance.

Neve scrounged up a round of applause, muffled by her gloves.

Isobel slid an arm around her shoulders and drew her in for a side hug. "We're going to miss you when you leave."

"I'm sure I'll come back to visit you." Sharing a child with Gil would necessitate trips from her home in North Carolina. Nerves seared her over navigating potentially tricky custody waters. "And I did get that extension until after the New Year to stick around for a while longer, to help you with Lottie's recovery after surgery."

As if Lottie hadn't faced enough challenges, she

now needed a kidney transplant due to complications from her spina bifida.

"I hope you know how much I appreciate that," Isobel said, her breath puffing clouds in the cold air. "I didn't want to ask, but it means so much to me. I'll breathe easier once the transplant is complete. And I'm sure Lottie will be thrilled to have her Aunt Neve stay over the holidays."

They'd all but given up hope after the first donor match became ill. Then, in a surprising miracle, they found an even better candidate. A long-lost relative. An adult, and luckily an adult could still donate to a child over two years old, as long as there was enough belly space.

Their grandmother's will revealed she'd given up a baby boy for adoption at birth. Her dying request had been for them to locate her son and give him the ring her long ago lover had gifted her.

Finding that long-lost relative had netted results.

And complications.

That man had later paid tribute to his own adoptive parents by opting to adopt a son. A *tempting* adopted son who'd turned Neve's world upside down from the moment she and Gil had met. As if things weren't convoluted enough, even though they weren't related by blood.

Well, except through the pregnancy.

She just hoped she could be half as good of a mom as her sister. "Lottie's a wonderful kid and you're such a great mother. You make it look effortless, even in the most difficult of times."

Isobel's cheeks puffed with a long exhale as she tugged her hood back up. "It's far from that, but thanks for the kudos. I'm thankful to have such a supportive family."

Neve knew her siblings would help in a heartbeat if needed, but the thought of asking made her chest go tight. She'd always considered herself a loner, an independent soul. That trait had become even further ingrained after she'd been diagnosed with an autoimmune disease a year ago. She hadn't told her sisters about the diagnosis. She hadn't wanted to add worry when the focus needed to be on her little niece's impending kidney transplant.

And truth be told, Neve had needed time to assimilate the health news along with the repercussions.

And now? Her world had become more complicated than ever, thanks to that fling with a certain thrill-seeking hotshot. Right on cue, Gil and his chestnut-colored horse raced past her, his hard muscled body tensed for action. His handsome face radiated competitiveness and excitement. He oozed charisma that had tempted her from the start.

With her sabbatical drawing to a close and the textbook all but complete, time was ticking down to tell Gil about the baby they'd made under the late-summer stars.

Gil Hadley swung the polo mallet with far more force than necessary to send the brilliant red ball sailing across the snowy field. But then, he needed the outlet for his frustration.

The breakup with Neve had been inevitable. Whoever said opposites attract had been spot on. They'd just failed to mention how all those differences would eventually tear them apart. Seeing Neve here on the sidelines threatened his focus as well as his resolve to keep his distance.

As he powered down the field on his favorite quarter horse, he caught sight of her sleek hair lifting in the wind, sweeping across her face, and making him ache to brush it aside, to linger. He could still feel the texture of the silky locks, the softness of her skin.

Would he be able to put her out of his mind once she left the Top Dog Dude Ranch? He hoped so, as they seemed to stumble over each other at every turn. Like today. But even the thought of her moving back to North Carolina made his chest go tight.

He enjoyed the thrill of a little chaos, but the world had piled on lately. Not just his ill-fated attraction to Neve. But with surprise news about his father. Not only was Gil adopted but his father was as well. Something his dad had never seen fit to mention, even though Gil had struggled with the loss of his biological mother when she gave him up at five years old.

His father's parentage had only come up during this past summer. When Gil had asked him why he hadn't shared about it sooner, River Jack had simply said he had chosen adoption as a tribute to the couple who adopted him from a teenage girl decades ago. Gil just wished his jeweler father would have told him before the news rippled through all of Moonlight Ridge. He'd let that frustration chip away at what had long been a hard-and-fast rule in his romantic life.

Never date happily-ever-after women. And Neve Dawson personified a white-picket-fence future. Never Neve? Was that his new motto?

His gaze slid over to her, taking his attention away from the game at just the wrong moment.

"Hey, Gil." Troy Shaw galloped past, riding a piebald paint. The former rodeo champ had a competitive streak a mile wide. "Get your brain back in the game and off the girl."

Gil hauled his gaze off Neve and back on the field—just as the ball skated past him, sailing into the goal.

For the other team.

He gritted his teeth in frustration. No need to even bother apologizing. The match had resumed and he had ground to regain, now that they were behind, thanks to him.

Gil narrowed his focus on the field of play, nudging his quarter horse back into the melee. "Ranger and I are all in, buddy. All in."

A motto he lived by. All In, or Not at All. He couldn't be that forever guy and he didn't want anyone hurt.

The pretty professor had been a major distraction since she'd arrived at the Top Dog Dude Ranch last summer. They'd enjoyed a brief affair, caught up in the revelry of a harvest-day celebration. But she'd ended things just as quickly, noting her job waiting for her in another state. Yet they kept bumping into each other, the attraction simmering, her prim but sassy professor vibe turning him inside out. Even now.

Having her on the sidelines weighed heavy on his conscience. How ironic that he was now tied to Neve forever since his father was about to donate a kidney to Neve's niece.

The thought of his dad's impending surgery sent a fresh wave of tension through Gil, made all the worse as the opposing team nailed another goal.

The Top Dog staff lost. By one goal. Which made the loss squarely his fault.

Sighing, he dismounted and smoothed a hand along Ranger's neck. "Good boy. I'll make sure you get an extra treat for keeping me seated during my pathetic performance this afternoon."

A shadow slid past him just as the ranch owner pulled up alongside him, leading his own blood bay thoroughbred by the reins. Jacob O'Brien grinned in greeting. "Well, Gil, as much as I hate losing, I have to admit you sure made the day for one of our most loyal guests."

"That wasn't my intent," Gil said wryly. "I'm sorry to have let my team down."

"Dude, you scored two out of three of our goals. I'd say you more than carried your weight."

"You can be assured I'll perform better during our next go-round, boss."

Jacob chuckled, shaking his head as he stroked his quarter horse. "Given you're one of the most competitive individuals I've ever met, I don't doubt that for a minute. All of us Top Dog longtimers are happy to have you on board. My wife's planning to take an afternoon off from the bakery to enjoy one of your snowshoeing expeditions."

"I appreciate the show of support. It'll be nice to make use of this heavier-than-usual snowfall." His list of activities for December had needed adjusting due to the unexpected storms that came early this year. But he'd welcomed the challenge.

He'd left a higher-paying job at a Wyoming resort to take this job. The spread out West had grown too "slick" for his liking. He preferred how, in spite of how large Top Dog grew, they stayed true to their rustic roots. It wasn't all about the bottom line. They made a living, but not at the expense of staying true to the land.

Jacob clapped a hand on his shoulder. "All joking aside. Are you doing okay, man?"

Not really. But venting as much wouldn't be wise.

The last thing he needed was to risk his job. He appreciated living close to his father, especially now. So he kept it simple. "I'm just worried about my dad." True enough. "I'll be relieved when the surgery is past."

"Of course you're concerned. Completely understandable. Take time off, if you need. We'll cover for you here."

"I appreciate that, but we're set. Luckily, Dad has agreed to have a nurse provide extra care through the holidays. Doc Barnett recommended her."

"Then, whoever she is, she'll be top-notch," Jacob nodded. "I'm glad to hear you're not carrying the weight of his care all on your own."

"Seems I'm not carrying much of it at all on my own. The ranch network is a supportive lot. It's already a tremendous help that the lodge dining hall will be sending over meals. Far healthier than whatever my bachelor skills would concoct. Campfire cooking is more my speed."

"We think the world of River Jack and what he's doing for Lottie." Jacob clapped a hand on his shoulder. "Well, I won't keep you any longer. Looks like you've got someone waiting to speak with you. I'll take your horse so you can head right over."

Gil almost questioned what Jacob meant, then he saw the direction of his boss's gaze. Straight to Neve. Gil rocked back on his boot heels.

Could she really be here for him after all these months of trying to avoid him? To be fair, a snow-polo match wasn't her normal outing so something—or someone—must have drawn her to this event.

A kick of excitement nailed him in the gut. Too much so. They'd ended their short-lived relationship because of their different lifestyles and her insistence on returning to North Carolina.

So why was she here, looking far too pretty in her red jacket with a forest green scarf? He certainly intended to find out.

* * *

By the end of the match, Neve's stomach grumbled with hunger.

She pressed a hand against her midsection as the two teams lined up to shake hands, the Top Dog group conceding defeat to the guest players. She'd skipped breakfast, other than a handful of crackers to settle her queasiness. Getting in sync with all the changes in her body hadn't been easy, and every day seemed to bring on a different set of symptoms. Her obstetrician reassured her not to worry. Still, she fretted because of her autoimmune disease.

Learning she had lupus a year ago had rocked her world, shifting the way she guarded her health and energy. Her boyfriend had bailed on her within days of her diagnosis. He'd babbled something about needing space and not being ready for anything serious. The breakup, along with the medical news, had also spurred her to apply for the sabbatical, to finish writing her textbook and give herself time to restructure her life for more downtime.

When she'd met Gil, she'd been wary, both in heart and mind. But his charm had won her over, for the short term at least. Now she'd made a tangle of things by not thinking through the consequences of a relationship when they had so little in common.

Isobel tugged her hood onto her head as the wind picked up. "What a shame they lost, but they seemed to have fun all the same. I'm going to talk with Cash for a bit before I head on back. Do you want to come along?"

Neve shook her head. "I'm going to stick around. But thanks. I'll meet with you later for making Christmas cookies."

Her stomach grumbled again.

Zelda tugged her parka zipper higher. "I'll be there with frosting and sprinkles. Are you okay here if I join Isobel?"

"Of course," Neve answered, thankful not to have to explain why she needed her to leave. "See you later."

As both of her sisters picked their way across the sludgy sidelines, Neve contrarily wished they'd lingered just a little longer so she didn't look so awkward, so *obvious*, standing around waiting for the opportunity to speak with Gil about the baby.

More and more familiar eyes turned in her direction. Nerves made her so itchy she searched for an exit route—only to have Gil's gaze meet hers. All thoughts of escape fled. In fact, all thoughts faded except for those focused on Gil. He'd pulled off the protective hard hat from the game, his light brown hair mussed and thick, making her fingers long to smooth the wayward locks back into place. But that was no longer wise or her right.

Leading his horse by the reins, Gil made a wide sweep around the crowd on his way toward her, stopping an arm's length away. "What did you think of the match?"

Her mouth went dry and she swallowed once, twice. "I've never heard of snow polo before. It was… interesting." She'd barely slept, thinking of seeing him today. He'd filled her dreams, even more than normal.

His low laugh rumbled a fresh cloud of white into the air between them. "Not much of a rousing endorsement."

"I thought it appeared dangerous, but then, that seems to be your prerequisite."

"I take safety seriously, for the participants and for the ranch's reputation."

"Of course," she answered, genuinely. Gil might be a risk-taker, but so far as she'd seen over the last few months, he was always a stickler for caution with the guests. "I'm sorry. Remember, though, that I'm more of a walk-in-the-woods kind of gal."

"I recall very well."

Her face heated with so many memories. Especially the time they detoured from a walk for a stolen moment alone in the boathouse. He'd tucked a chair under the doorknob so no one could interrupt. They'd made love against the wall with the scent of cedar filling her gasping breaths. Every time she passed that building by the lake, heat flushed her face.

But they'd taken other strolls as well, without veering off the path. Hand in hand, they'd clocked miles in the woods, talking about nature and dreams. Those meandering treks tormented her as much, if not more, than the passionate interludes.

She pushed away distracting thoughts and focused

on the present. "Would you mind taking one of those walks with me—no detours," she rushed to add. "After you've put your horse away, of course."

"How about now? I can lead Ranger along with us since your place isn't far from the stables anyway."

"That would be great." She offered a wobbly smile, resenting the nerves.

In her academic world, she was in control, confident. But when it came to relationships? She struggled.

With each step, she drew in icy cold breaths to still her nerves. Dense walls of pine trees lined the path, boughs glistening with a light sheen of ice. Moonlight Ridge had been beautiful in June, when she'd arrived. But now? In the winter? The countryside was magnificent, glistening with nature's holiday decor. Although the ranch had added their own touches as well, with twinkling lights in the branches and the occasional clusters of iron dogs.

"What brings you here? I wouldn't have thought snow polo would be your preferred entertainment."

"You would be correct in that assumption. Actually, I've been trying to track you down." No matter how many breaths she took, the nerves increased, making her woozy. She'd practiced her speech a million times in her mind, but now that the time neared, she craved more time. "I, uh, need to chat with you about, um, something."

"I'm all ears," he said, patting Ranger's neck.

"So is everyone else here." She nodded toward the

clusters of people, half of whom were already looking in their direction. Gossip would spread soon enough. She'd pushed her luck waiting this long. "I'd prefer to talk away from eavesdroppers."

Nodding, he gestured toward a fork in the path that led toward her cabin. Sunlight filtered through the trees, dappling the ground. The crisp evergreen scent filled the air. Oaks and pines lined the narrow trail, with pawprint-shaped markers pointing the way to cabins, the main lodge, the stables, and so on. Each guest received a ranch app when they arrived with a list of activities and a legend map, but the cell phone service could be spotty.

Gil held Ranger's lead, the horse walking on one side of him, Neve on the other. "This sounds serious. Especially since we've barely spoken in two months." His deep brown eyes held a gentle censure.

"I'm sorry for that." It had just been so difficult to be around him and still hold on to her resolve not to jump right back into a fling. Once she'd started to catch feels, she'd known she had to stop. She couldn't face another man walking away because of her health issues. "I truly didn't mean to be rude."

"You've been unfailingly…polite. But standoffish."

"It seemed best once we realized our, uh, fling had run its course." Even saying the words aloud made her dizzy.

"I wouldn't say the attraction had fizzled out," he said dryly.

"Let me rephrase." She pressed a hand to her forehead, searching for the right way to tell him about the pregnancy. "It seemed wise to keep my distance once we realized our affair couldn't lead anywhere."

He scrubbed a hand over his jawline. "I wish things didn't have to be so awkward. The ranch is a small community..."

"Uh-huh." She struggled to focus on his voice, but the hunger pangs kept hitting her harder and harder, increasing the dizziness.

She braced a hand on tree trunk for balance, the iciness leeching through her glove. Carefully, she continued—

And slid along a slick patch of ice.

Her arms shot out as her heart lurched in her chest. The world spun, but in a slow-motion way as she searched for something, anything to grab onto. Her fist slid along a branch too slick to hold.

Gil caught her just as her feet went out from under her. He hauled her to his chest. She looked up into his face, a fresh wave of vertigo washing over her.

Except this time, the wooziness had nothing to do with her diet and everything to do with the warm wall of his muscular chest.

Chapter Two

Worry knocked Gil for a loop.

His arms locked tighter around Neve and he searched her face for signs of illness. Her eyes were hazy but she was conscious.

His heart hammered in his chest. He braced his boots, grateful for the good treads that kept him from slipping or dropping her. Thank heaven he'd caught her before she took a nasty spill on the ice. He didn't even want to think about what might have happened had she been out here on one of her nature walks all alone.

Not that he intended to bring that up now. He'd given up any rights to chime in about her life. Better to focus on the here and now.

Although with the tempting minty scent of her shampoo, he found his own world was far from steady. Finally, he held her in his arms again. He'd missed her. More than he wanted to admit.

He willed his pulse to sync up with the slow *drip, drip, drip* of a melting icicle.

Clasping her shoulders, he eased back a step carefully, already missing the feel of her in his arms. "Are you okay? You almost fainted."

"Just a little bit woozy. I didn't eat much for breakfast." She pressed a gloved hand to her stomach. "Thanks for the rescue."

"I'm glad I was here to catch you." He winced as soon as the words were out of his mouth. They'd had more than one argument on the subject during their short relationship. A can of mace and a bear whistle couldn't tackle all the dangers off the beaten trail. He might be a risk-taker, but he also was a firm believer in the buddy system and safety, making him worry about how much time she spent alone in the woods.

Her mouth went tight.

He rushed to add, "I'm sure you've been burning the candle at both ends lately, finishing up your textbook manuscript. And I know your sister appreciates the help right now, but you need to take care of yourself too."

She flinched at his words. "I'll keep that in mind."

Had she chafed at what she deemed his *overprotectiveness*? He wasn't sure and wondered if he'd wrecked the opportunity to chat with her, an opening she'd initiated. He reached to brush away a strand of hair streaking across her face, savoring the texture as he searched for the right words.

Then a movement just past her shoulder caught his attention. A pair of birds flapped from an icy branch toward the trio of sister cabins. All three glowed with holiday cheer, from the twinkling lights in the bushes to the single, decorative candles in the windows. Each door sported a wreath and fat red bow.

Yet each carried a touch of individuality. Isobel's cabin sported a Santa Paws, Please Stop Here sign by the picket fence. Zelda's cabin had an iron rocking horse out front, no doubt a nod to her rodeo fiancé. And Neve? A pair of decorated bird houses were staked on either side of the front porch steps.

Just as he started to ask her why she wanted to talk, he caught sight of her sisters walking toward their cabins. They must have taken the longer trail with its flatter, wider path. Isobel pushed Lottie's wheelchair along the cleared walkway, not an easy task in the winter, even with her special tires. They bypassed their own cottages and made a beeline toward Neve's.

Disappointment and relief jockeyed inside him. On the one hand, he hated to see the time together end, but on the other, he needed time to get his head together. Their breakup had hit him harder than it should for a short-term fling.

Gil shifted his attention back to the enticing woman beside him. "Looks like you have company, so I won't keep you."

"Company?" Her face creased with confusion. She pivoted and he palmed her waist before he could think.

"Just making sure you don't slip again," he justified, remembering the days when they didn't think twice about touching each other.

She smiled at him, her blue eyes sparkling. "Thanks." She glanced back at her home again. "I can't believe I let time slip away from me. My sisters and I planned to bake cookies this afternoon—we're participating in a cookie exchange tomorrow. I thought we were supposed to meet at Isobel's to bake though."

"Maybe they're just coming to get you." He kept his hand on her waist, the two of them staying by the dense tree line of evergreens, extending their time together since her sisters hadn't noticed them yet. "Could I pay you to bake extra so I can attend this exchange too? My baking repertoire steers mostly to campfire meals."

The words took on a life of their own, filling the air with memories of the evening they'd camped by the river. He'd cooked a pizza in a cast-iron skillet and they'd sipped wine as the stars flickered to light the night sky.

Her breathing hitched, her chest moving faster. "There are plenty of folks who would be happy to trade for one of your Dutch oven cinnamon rolls."

So she did remember that night, and the next morning as they'd eaten pastries and licked the frosting off each other's fingers.

He cleared his throat, wishing clearing his mind of the haze of desire could be as easy. "What was it you wanted to talk to me about?"

Chewing her bottom lip, she looked from him to her cabin with her siblings in the yard, then back again. "Can we reschedule the chat? My sisters are waiting and I would rather we speak at a time we won't be interrupted. Would you mind meeting me at the bonfire gathering tonight? So we can continue our talk without being overheard?"

He searched her face, her furrowed brow giving him pause. "That's still mighty public."

"We can find a quiet spot, or you could walk me home afterward."

That frown of hers kept him from reading too much into her words. "I'll see you there."

Her eyes held his for a moment, her blue eyes wide before she turned away.

"Neve?" he called after her. "Don't forget to eat."

She waved a hand over her shoulder in acknowledgment.

Grinning, he watched her as she picked her way back toward the cabin. Even swaddled in a thick parka she tempted him, making him ache to peel away those layers.

Her senses still alive from the feel of Gil's arms around her, Neve followed her sisters from her cabin to Isobel's after they'd come searching for her. She could feel the questioning weight of their gazes as they worked together in a pseudo assembly line.

The kitchen swirled with warmed scents of cinnamon, vanilla, and sugar, taking her back to childhood memories of baking with Gran. They'd included Lottie today, as well as Zelda's future stepdaughter, Harper, passing on the holiday baking tradition. Neve wanted her child to have memories like these.

Blinking back emotional tears, yet another side effect of this new pregnancy, she let the familiar music of their voices circle around her as she pulled a fresh pan of sugar cookies from the oven. No doubt her siblings wondered about finding her with Gil earlier. They didn't know about the brief affair, but they'd commented more than once about their charged interactions, asking if there might be something between them.

Regardless, she couldn't tell them about the baby before informing Gil.

She also couldn't eat the raw cookie dough that was currently calling her name from the inside of a bowl. Raw eggs were a big no-no during pregnancy. So of course she craved all things cookie dough. So, there was nothing left to do but start decorating the cooled ones on the rack.

Neve reached for a tub of frosting from beside a mug full of candy canes, admiring the way Isobel's cozy cabin felt a little magical with all the holiday decorations. From the decorated noble fir in one corner to the simple pine garland draped through an antler chandelier, the homey touches reminded Neve of all she hadn't done to prepare for Christmas. "I feel like a decorating slacker in comparison to the rest of you."

Her sisters outlined patterns on the cookies with thin streams of colored icing, while Zelda's future stepdaughter and Lottie poured sprinkles on another batch.

Isobel set aside the tube of snowflake blue and

said softly, "We got a head start to finish up all our holiday prep before Lottie's surgery. I'm almost done decorating and even managed to freeze some extra cookie dough."

"Of course." Neve glanced across the room at her niece, who had her tongue sticking out of the corner of her mouth as she concentrated on a stocking-shaped treat. "I wish I'd thought to come help you with the early start. I should have realized…"

She'd been so wrapped up in her own concerns, she'd missed the changes in her sister's place. Now she looked around with fresh eyes. Dog-themed ornaments filled the live tree in the corner, lights twinkling. Plaid stockings hung from the mantel, including a bone-shaped one in matching fabric. For Cocoa, of course.

A stone fireplace stretched to the high ceiling, the air carrying the scent of a crackling fire as well as fresh garland, compliments of the neighboring Christmas-tree farm. Log walls, pine and leather furniture rounded out the decor.

Fairy lights hung on the dog-themed signs. A plaque on a stand beside the sofa proclaimed I Love You Furever. A massive piece of driftwood spread over the mantel with painted lettering: Stay Paws-itive. And above the archway framing the hall, another sign was etched with Anything is Paws-ible.

The place felt like something out of a magazine promoting a getaway holiday, complete with modifications for Lottie. The doors were wider to accommodate a wheelchair, perfect as Lottie finished a snowman shaped cookie, her squeal of delight echoing to the rafters. The kitchen counter was lower in places where Lottie could roll right up without having to reach awkwardly. The bathrooms sported rails and an accessible shower. And the list went on and on. Such simple—and crucial—additions that could make or break a home for Lottie.

"I wish Gran and our parents could be here to celebrate with us. It's every bit as wonderful of a little town as Gran told us growing up."

Isobel rolled her eyes. "Once I got over my fear of driving through the mountains."

Zelda elbowed her, jingle-bell earrings swaying. "When do you drive? Seems to me we chauffer you or you're on horseback."

"Guilty as charged." Isobel relented with a grin as she pressed two candy eyes on a gingerbread man.

Neve angled over to look at Zelda's progress on a cookie. "What shape is that?"

Zelda held up the cutter she'd brought. "It's a dog."

"But what's…? Oh my." Neve clapped a hand over her mouth, unsure whether to be appalled or amused.

The dog pattern showed a pup from behind. Leave it to Zelda to make a bunch of dog butts. Isobel licked batter off the spoon.

Neve's mouth watered with a craving that rivaled even her midnight yearning for rocky road ice cream.

Isobel offered her the bowl. "There's a good scrape left if you want."

"No thanks." Neve shook her head.

Her sister nudged it closer. "Are you sure? You were always the first in line to lick the spoon when we were growing up."

The last thing Neve needed was questions that would lead to suspicions. Her siblings were intuitive, especially Isobel. Neve reached for a Hershey Kiss from the bowl beside the peanut butter dough and peeled the foil off the candy.

As the milk chocolate melted on her tongue, it wasn't as good as cookie dough, but at least she'd stopped her sister's questions.

For now.

Gil swung the axe toward the log, with extra heft, splitting the wood in half. Exercise and hard work had always helped him burn off frustration in the past. He was about half a cord in, and he wasn't anywhere close to settled.

He pitched the two pieces on the growing pile near the roaring bonfire for tonight's event. His buddies Troy and Cash were chopping alongside, adding to the growing stack needed for such a cold evening.

A couple dozen attendees were already gathered, with many more making their way over from the lodge. Guests strolled past the ice skating rink with a massive Christmas tree in the middle. Oversize ornaments decorated the boughs with orbs, stars, and snowflake shapes.

The smell of roasting hot dogs mingled with the

hint of smoke. An old chuck wagon was parked off to the side, serving hot dogs, chili, and the makings for s'mores, along with hot chocolate and warmed cider.

He rolled another log from the back of the truck bed, positioned it, then put his all into bringing down the axe. He'd been on edge this afternoon since his walk with Neve. In part because of her near fall. And also because he could have sworn that she swayed toward him, that her eyes glistened with attraction.

Would she still show up tonight for whatever she wanted to discuss in private? Not that he was sure how he would react if she wanted to renew their affair.

Aw, man, who was he kidding? If she invited him back into her bed, he would set a land-speed record racing up the trail to her place.

"Hey, bud," Troy called from the other nearby chopping block. "Slow down, or I'll have to keep up and I'm already winded."

Chuckling, Gil set aside his axe and stacked the extra logs. "I'm just holding up my end of the work."

He enjoyed the camaraderie he'd found with the other staff and families here. To be honest, he'd hoped Neve would change her mind and stick around. No such luck. Neve had been clear about returning to her teaching job. Although surely she would come back here to visit her sisters.

Zelda was engaged to the ranch's own resident rodeo champ who had just opened a training center nearby. For now, he rented a cabin on the ranch while his house was built behind the facility.

Troy tugged his work gloves on more securely. "So, are the two of you still pretending you're not an item?"

Gil gathered up a handful of wood shavings to use as kindling later. He didn't need the added pressure of gossip. "I don't have a clue what you're talking about."

Snorting on a laugh, Cash swiped the back of his arm along the sweat beading along his forehead. "Yeah, right. Nobody's buying that line. The chemistry between the two of you just about melts the snow."

"Well, I can assure you both, there's nothing going on with Neve and me." Not now, anyway. Then a notion tugged at him, making him wonder. "Why? Have her sisters been saying something otherwise?"

Cash nudged over the crate for kindling. "Just standard Top Dog gossip-mill stuff, for the most part. The sisters are close though. So I've heard bits and pieces through Isobel. You may have noticed they can be quite the romantics."

Troy nodded. "That makes sense, given their fairy-tale names."

Gil looked over at the trio of sisters as they chatted it up with Santa making his rounds. "Their what?"

"Fairy-tale names," Troy repeated. "You know, because of their grandmother's influence."

How had he not heard this before? "I'm not sure what you mean."

Cash set the kindling box on top of the woodpile. "Isobel, as in Belle from *Beauty and the Beast*. Which is fitting, given that she's a writer, her world filled with words and books. It's kismet that she and I were friends, like in that story, before we became a couple." Isobel was divorced from her first husband, Lottie's father.

"And Zelda?" Gil asked, glancing at Troy.

"Rapun-Zel," Troy said with an affectionate grin.

Gil chuckled. "And now she grooms dog hair, or rather fur. Cute." Which brought him to the question he cared about most. "What about Neve?"

Cash leaned against the truck's tailgate. "Apparently, there's some tie into Neve meaning *snow* in some of the romance languages. Like Snow White, and now she spends her days wandering the woods studying nature and wildlife. I've often wondered if the names steered them to their chosen professions. Or if they were prophetic—their grandmother was from Moonlight Ridge, after all. Now the sisters are here and two of them plan to stay."

The vision of Neve as Snow White sure hadn't missed the mark by much. She knew a lot about wildlife, easily spotting the tiny tracks of the bird species she wrote about in her research paper, always careful not to disturb the creatures she studied.

Gil scrubbed a hand over his forehead as if to banish the fanciful thoughts. "For now. But Neve will be a few hundred miles away after New Year's."

Cash frowned, scrubbing a hand along his neck. "How do you feel about that?"

Conflicted?

Confused?

Part of him wanted to wave goodbye, no strings

when she left. And another part of him suspected forgetting her wouldn't be that simple. That, for a long while to come, he would look for her around every corner.

Gil settled for a simpler answer that would hopefully end the conversation. "How do I feel? There's nothing to note. We saw each other for a short while. We didn't want to tell anyone because of gossip around this place. Things didn't work out. Time to move on."

Easier said than done. Hopefully distance would help with the temptation once she moved back to North Carolina after the new year.

Troy straightened, angling to look past them. "Is that your father?"

Thankful for the diversion, Gil set aside his axe and peered into the darkness lit by electric tiki torches along the path. Sure enough, his dad ambled over on snowshoes, whereas last year, he would have opted for an ATV. River Jack had worked overtime on improving his health in these months leading up to the kidney donation. Between the daily exercise and tightening up his diet, he'd dropped weight and lowered his blood pressure.

Gil admired his dad for his selflessness. At the same time, Gil worried for his dad's health. He loved his old man and worried with each day he crossed off the calendar bringing them closer to the surgery date. He would trade places with his father if he could, except he hadn't been a match. But then he wasn't biologically related to Lottie the way his father was, so the odds of Gil being a donor had been lower.

"Hey there, gentlemen." River Jack leaned against a pine tree as he unbuckled his snowshoes. "Do you need a helping hand?"

Grinning, Gil buried his axe blade in a log so it wouldn't lie around loose. "Now, didn't you time that just right? We've just finished up with the chopping. Nothing left to do now but stack, and that shouldn't take us long."

River Jack set the snowshoes in the truck bed. "Alrighty, then. If you're sure you don't need me, I'll head over to chat with Lottie and her family. Maybe I'll even chat with Santa Claus about my wish for this Christmas."

Gil's gaze darted across the lawn, past the crackling flames toward the woman who was never far from his thoughts these days. Her hair tumbled over her shoulder in a dark splash. And her trim legs in jeans had him remembering the feel of her satiny skin. He still didn't have a clue what Neve wanted to speak with him about, but he knew the cookout couldn't end soon enough for his liking.

Chapter Three

Neve wondered why no one had ever shared about raging hormones during pregnancy. The longer she'd stared at Gil chopping firewood for the cookout gathering, the more she burned inside to renew their affair. Something she absolutely could not afford to do. Her baby needed her to stay levelheaded, no chaos of on-again, off-again relationships. Especially not with Gil when they needed to navigate the tricky terrain of custody and parenting. The best thing she could do was offer her baby stability.

Still, there was no harm in just looking. She wasn't the only one riveted by the sight, including her sisters, standing on either side of her as the ranch owners gave their welcome spiel to new guests around the bonfire.

"Welcome to Moonlight Ridge, Tennessee, home of the Top Dog Dude Ranch and the magical Sulis Cave… When my wife Hollie and I founded the Top Dog Dude Ranch, we planned for it to be more than a vacation spot. We wanted to create a haven, a place of refuge with tools available to enhance your life. It's our hope that through our enrichment 'pack-tivities' you carry a piece of the Top Dog experience with you when you return home…"

As Jacob continued with the speech she'd grown familiar with over the past few months, the words grew faint to Neve as she shifted her attention back to Gil…

He stacked the firewood closer to the bonfire, showing no signs of slowing, even though he'd also split all those giant logs with powerful strength. But those hands could also be so incredibly gentle.

Why did she have to be this attracted to a guy so completely wrong for her? And why did he have to torture her by performing the hottest form of manual labor?

His tirelessness only showcased another hurdle they would have had to overcome. She could never keep up with him, not with her health constraints. Ending their relationship had been difficult for her, but not nearly as tough as it would be to have him walk away out of boredom from her simple, ivory-tower lifestyle.

Man, what a holiday buzzkill.

Zelda fanned her face, somehow making a candy-cane-striped snowsuit look stylish in her own unconventional way. "Have mercy, that vision is so hot, they could sell tickets."

Isobel pressed her gloved hand to her forehead. "Guests would line up for that. Maybe we should tell the ranch owners to add a couple of photos to the website. What do you think?"

Neve adjusted her scarf to disguise her fidgeting—

and give herself time to unstick her tongue from the roof of her mouth. "Jacob and Hollie really went all out this evening. I expected a festive air, but this is all next level without seeming kitschy."

Christmas carols drifted from the sound system. A pair of kids held hands as they skipped past singing "Jingle Bells." Winter coats and boots were accessorized with bright holiday scarves and gloves. The ranch also supplied a basket filled with snowy-white knit mittens and hats for anyone who lost theirs throughout the evening.

Nodding, Isobel extended her gloved hands out to warm in front of the fire. "I agree. I'm reminded of how the Top Dog Dude Ranch promotes itself as being a place to restore and recharge."

A cast-iron pot rested on the grate, filled with water, cinnamon, cranberries, and oranges steaming the yummiest of scents into the air. Her heightened sense of smell still caught her by surprise. Right now, at least, in a pleasant way.

Zelda rubbed her gloved palms together near the fire. "I could smell the potpourri—and simmering chili—all the way in the grooming salon. An interesting blend of flavors, but the dogs in the shop were salivating."

"So was I." A voice drifted over an instant before Lottie wheeled her chair closer to her mom. "How much longer until supper?"

Cocoa trotted alongside, wearing red plaid booties and a matching scarf. His green vest proclaimed his service-dog status with a reminder not to pet. The chocolate Labrador retriever focused all his attention on his young charge, their bond unmistakable.

Isobel passed a cup of hot chocolate to her daughter. "Only a few more minutes. Maybe some hot cocoa will help you wait."

"Cocoa, like my dog's brown fur," Lottie said with a giggle and smiled her thanks. "Can I give this one to Jack? He's heading our way. I can get another one for myself."

Isobel rested a hand on her shoulder. "Sure, sweetie, I'll go get it right now. You just stay here with Aunt Neve and Aunt Zelda. If they don't mind?"

Neve rushed to assure her, "Of course, I'm happy to hang out with my favorite niece."

And yes, that would keep her closer to Gil. She needed to learn to manage her reaction to the man, now that they were connected for life through their child. Right? Except she was also making excuses for herself.

"River Jack," Lottie squealed, waving with one hand while holding the cocoa in her other.

The older gentleman waved in return, looking festive in his red plaid trapper-style hat, with earflaps. River Jack was shorter than his son, although since they weren't biologically related the differences in their appearance weren't a surprise. However, they shared many of the same mannerisms. Like a smile that lit the eyes, the sound of their laugh, and the way they made friends with everyone.

Lottie extended the steaming cup, cradled in her candy-apple-red gloves. "Hey there, Mr. River Jack. I got some hot cocoa for you. Cocoa, like my service dog's name…" She giggled. "It's funny."

He knelt in front of her wheelchair. "This is exactly what I needed after my walk over here. What a smart and thoughtful girl you are."

"We're friends." Lottie passed him the cocoa, whipped cream floating with peppermint sprinkles on top. "That's what pals do for each other. Isn't that right, Aunt Neve?"

Neve smoothed a hand over Lottie's knit hat, adjusting the pom-pom on top. "You're absolutely correct, kiddo. Your mama taught you well."

How could she not be touched by the sweet exchange? This man would be her child's grandfather. His or her only grandparent. Thinking of how much Gran had meant to her and her sisters, Neve wanted to hug River Jack hard. She could blame the emotions on pregnancy, but the power and beauty of how this all played out would move anyone with a beating heart.

The final piece of Gran's wishes would be complete this Christmas when they gave River Jack the ring his biological father had given Gran all those years ago. A ring made with a crystal from the Sulis Cave in Moonlight Ridge. And now, River Jack made jewelry using more of those gems.

A shiver, the mystical kind, rippled through Neve. Some of the famed Moonlight Ridge magic? Except that usually involved a dog or other animal somehow.

Now she was being as fanciful as Gran, instead of a scientist of nature.

Lottie shifted her attention back to the older man. "Are you working on any new jewelry? Do you just use red and white and green crystals this time of year?"

Taking a quick sip of his hot chocolate, River Jack stood. "Yes, ma'am, I'm working on fresh pieces, but all colors. Whatever the order calls for. It's Christmastime, so I'm getting all my orders ready."

"Before we get our surgery, right?" The child chewed her bottom lip.

"I'll have my work done by then so I can enjoy the holiday recovering," he answered before leaning forward conspiratorially. "But I'm also hoping to pass the time sketching some new items. I'll share a sketch and you can color a photo for me. It'll be a great way to pass the time while we get better."

"Sure, but I've been saving my allowance to buy a real piece of jewelry." Lottie scrunched her freckled nose, red-tipped from the cold. "How much does a necklace cost?"

"I'm happy to make a custom order for you. Just describe what you want."

The little girl leaned forward, her eyes earnest as her voice lowered. "It's actually for my mommy. So I should pay for it. Besides, you're already doing a lot for me."

Neve's heart squeezed and she swiped away a tear

gathering in the corner of her eye. Her emotions seemed so very close to the surface these days.

His face grew somber and he clasped her hands. "Hey, kiddo, please don't ever feel like you owe me anything. I want to do this. And someday, you'll do something for someone else. And they'll do a favor for another person. It's called paying it forward."

Neve rested a hand on Lottie's shoulder again. "Paying it forward. I like that—"

Her phone chimed with an incoming text. The distinctive chime reminded her she hadn't changed the ringtone she'd chosen for Gil's messages. She shot a nervous look at River Jack, not that he would know her ringtone code.

Her stomach flipped as she tugged her cell from her coat pocket and read…

Looking forward to our walk after the cookout. We need to talk before you leave.

Her gaze snapped back to where she'd seen him last. He stood by the woodpile with his phone in his hand, but his eyes held hers. Intently.

Her mouth went dry and her breath hitched. Did he suspect? Had somebody tipped him off? But who? She hadn't even told her sisters and she couldn't imagine her doctor would break confidentiality.

Three deep breaths later, she calmed herself and told her imagination to have a seat in the time-out corner. Her plan to tell Gil first was still on track.

* * *

River Jack Hadley had been searching for a reason to wake up in the morning since he'd lost his wife. At first, he'd hung on for his son, and most days, he still did. But every now and again, the grief sucker punched him.

Hard.

On one of those days he'd heard about the little girl's search for a kidney donor and he'd thought maybe, just maybe, that would give his life meaning. In making the decision to be tested, he hadn't expected to find a whole new family, as well as the answer to his parentage.

Life sure was strange.

He sipped his hot chocolate, eyeing the food wagon parked beyond the bonfire. The flames licked toward the sky, crackling a warm blaze that took the edge off the crisp mountain air.

Angling sideways, he made his way past a duo singing holiday tunes, encouraging others to join in. He enjoyed the live-music offerings, a surprise perk of attending Top Dog functions. And in a cost-effective manner too. A variety of employees comprised a pickup band they called Raise the Woof. Participants varied, but the quality never wavered.

He paused in front of the garland-strung food buffet, scanning the offerings for the healthiest. He intended to make sure he was in the best of condition for the transplant procedure. He bypassed the hot dogs and settled on a turkey burger with crisp, fire-braised corn. One of those fruit skewers wouldn't be too shabby for dessert. He could all but hear his late wife laughing in his ear, the selections being far from his diet in years past.

Turning with his plate, he stopped short just before bumping into a woman, an unfamiliar face. Maybe a new guest?

"Pardon me," he said. "I'm afraid my taste buds distracted me."

"No harm, no foul," she answered lightheartedly, adjusting her knit beret.

"Please don't let me keep you from you from enjoying your dinner." When he looked over her shoulder, she appeared to be alone.

His focus slid back to her. He studied her more closely, finding her a pretty lady in a long forest-green jacket, with black boots and a knit beret. Some might think she was overdressed for a bonfire, but she exuded a confidence that made it all work. Or maybe it was that her clothes were updated versions of styles from another generation. His. And possibly hers too.

And for the first time in a very long time, he was intrigued. Not just attracted or interested. But *intrigued*. He set his plate and drink on a nearby picnic table. "If you're not waiting on someone, could I get you something to drink? I highly recommend the hot cocoa."

She looked over her shoulder then back at him before pointing to her chest. "Who, me?"

"Yes, ma'am, pretty lady." The flirtatious words

fell out of their own volition. Surprising. "I don't see anyone else around. Of course that could be your shining beauty dimming out the rest of the world."

Her eyes went wide for an instant before she burst into laughter.

He clapped a hand over his heart. "You've wounded me."

Her green eyes glinted with mischievousness. "Somehow, I believe you'll survive. And if the wound is too deep, then take assurance in the fact that I'm a nurse."

The spark of interest grew. His wife had been the love of his life, no question. Still, he tried to move forward, dated every now and again. But those relationships eventually fizzled.

Right now, he felt something far different than he'd experienced before. Something…special. "Good to know. How long are you vacationing here at the ranch?"

"Oh, you misunderstand." She filled a cup with cocoa and took a seat at the picnic table where he'd placed his food. "I live here."

"You do?" he asked, confused but glad for the opportunity to extend the conversation. "So do I. Well, not at the ranch exactly. I have a cabin nearby, but I work at the ranch as does my son, so I'm here a good bit. How have we not met yet?"

"I only just arrived in Moonlight Ridge a couple of weeks ago." She rubbed her hands together as if to warm them, even though she wore leather gloves.

She appeared more than a little out of his league. Not that he intended to back away until she gave a clear indication that she wanted him to move along. "How are you liking it so far?"

"Who wouldn't love this idyllic place?" She smiled and her green eyes lit with reflections from the fire. "It's like Tennessee's own little *Brigadoon*. That's my favorite play, although I've watched the movie version at least a half dozen times while sitting up with patients."

"Patients?" Then he remembered her saying she was a nurse. And new to the area, working at the ranch. A sense of foreboding crept up his spine.

He wondered if she could be...

Isobel interrupted his thoughts.

"Have you met Priscilla Kincaid?" Isobel hooked arms with him. "She is a nurse with Company Keepers and fills in at the clinic on occasion. I sure wish she had been here back when Lottie had the flu last month."

Her illness had further delayed the transplant.

The pieces came together in his mind with a miserable clarity. Torpedoing all thoughts of a special encounter with someone new. This wasn't just any nurse. Priscilla Kincaid would be *his* nurse during recovery. "It's nice to meet you, ma'am. I'm River Jack Hadley. I've heard them sing your praises."

And now this lady was going to see him at his absolute weakest, bringing him his meals and a bedpan. Now, that seriously killed the chemistry vibe.

* * *

The bonfire smoldered with the end of the cookout and Gil was no closer to figuring out why Neve had sought him out.

Now, as he walked her home, the stars dotted the inky night sky. The crisp air whispered through the branches. He loved his home state and couldn't imagine living anywhere else. Especially during the Christmas season, with the snowcapped mountains and glistening branches. He just hoped he would be celebrating his father's successful surgery before Christmas.

And would he see Neve as well? His father had mentioned doing a meal with Lottie's family, health permitting, to celebrate their connection. He glanced at Neve walking beside him, her lovely face scrunched in deep thought. She nibbled on the last of a s'more with a bliss that made him smile…and ache to lick a remnant of marshmallow from the corner of her mouth.

As quick as the thought came, he remembered her almost passing out earlier because of forgetting breakfast. A chill settled in his gut.

While he normally didn't mind quiet in the wilderness, he didn't want to waste what time he had with her, and already, he could see her cabin in the distance. He searched for something to say that could launch a conversation. "Have you finished your gift shopping yet?"

Her eyes went wide with surprise. She chewed fast and gulped. "Have you?"

"Yes ma'am," he said, proud to answer even if this was the first time for him. Ever. "Sure have."

Her laughter created tiny puffs of cloudy air and sent a rabbit scampering into the underbrush. "I thought that men waited until the day before Christmas to hit the stores."

"To be fair…" he answered with a grin, his boots crunching along the icy path. He'd missed her witty comebacks. "That's usually the case for me. This year, I wanted to get ahead of the curve so I'm available for my dad during his recovery."

"That's the very best present you could give him." She touched his arm lightly, only for an instant, before pulling back, but her touch lingered even through his winter coat. "Although from what I heard, he has a great nurse lined up—not that he or she could replace family, of course."

The weight of worry for his old man crept up on him again, and too easily, he could go full speed into those fears, like careening down a slope, heading for a wall of pine trees. He couldn't face the thought of a world without his dad, especially after losing his bio mom and adopted mom. He usually managed better to live in the present. Maybe Neve's fainting spell had his imagination working overtime.

They reached her white picket fence and he shoved the concerns to the back of his mind to unpack later. "You still haven't answered my question."

"I have finished my shopping, for pretty much the same reason. I want to help my sister with Lottie's recovery." She glanced over at him through eyelashes spiked with snowflakes as she swung open the gate.

"Any favorite picks? When I was growing up, we always chose the most inspired or thoughtful present," he asked, because he wanted to keep hearing the sound of her voice. And yes, he was curious what she valued, even as he wondered why he'd never thought to ask before.

"My gifts are all the same—sorta." She paused as a whitetail doe sprinted past, followed by two fawns, maybe six months old. "I printed out photos of each person from our time here and partnered it with a freshly pressed flower or leaf that accents the background. I framed them in the craft shop."

"That sounds pretty as well as thoughtful." He wondered what photo and pressing she would have chosen for him, if they'd still been together. "If you haven't wrapped them yet, I'd enjoy taking a look."

She gave him a schoolmarmish look, the moon streaming down on her pale face and upturned nose. "Are you asking me to invite you in to see my etchings?"

"Are you inviting me?" he asked, only halfway teasing as he tipped his head toward her cabin. There had been a time they'd snuck off together during every free moment alone. Sometimes, to her cabin full of textbooks. Other times, to his sparse, barely occupied place.

Until she'd started to worry that people might think they were a couple. He hadn't seen the harm in enjoying their time together until she left.

She'd insisted they were delaying the inevitable.

Her smile faded as she picked along the final few steps to her cabin and leaned against the porch post. "I'm afraid that wouldn't be a good idea. We have something important to discuss."

"I'm all ears." Curiosity had been eating him up all evening. He braced a boot on the bottom step.

He was fresh out of ideas about what she wanted to talk to him about, considering he'd pinned all hopes on her wanting to pick up where they left off three months ago. The fact that she hadn't invited him inside nipped that possibility in the bud.

"I wish there was an easy way to say this…"

Her hands shook and he reached to warm them between his. "Neve, you're worrying me. What's going on?"

The silence stretched between them for a dozen or so heartbeats until that concern started to build again. For a man who prided himself on his fearlessness, he had precious little skill at navigating the anxiety.

A barn owl screeched through the night and he jolted.

"Neve?" he repeated, squeezing her gloved hands lightly, urging her to talk to him.

She drew in a deep breath, then blurted, "I'm pregnant and you're the father."

Chapter Four

Growing up, Neve had dreamed of having kids one day. She'd imagined that special moment when she would tell her husband the happy news.

Telling the father of her child for real was not turning out remotely like her fantasies.

Pulse pounding, she waited for him to say something. Anything.

Gil simply stared at her, unblinking, his face devoid of expression, schooled in a way that revealed nothing. But even that relayed far too much. If he'd been happy, that would have overflowed. There would have been no reason to hide emotion from her. But the yellow moon overhead illuminated his face well enough.

Disappointment squeezed her heart, for herself and for her child. But for that baby's sake, Neve stayed on the porch with her teeth chattering from the cold rather than run into her cabin and slam the door in his face. No matter how things went between them, she needed to maintain communications lines.

Gil cleared his throat, tipping his head to the side.

"Could you repeat that, please? I'm not certain I heard you correctly."

Anger crackled inside her. She was pretty sure her diction had been crystal clear. All the same, she said—again, "I'm pregnant. The baby is yours. I know we used birth control, but it's not foolproof. And yes, you are the only person who could be the father."

"I wouldn't have suggested otherwise," he said indignantly. "I just need a minute to wrap my brain around the news."

She understood. She truly did. How long had she gaped at that pregnancy test when the first positive result stared her in the face? And yet, she couldn't deny she'd hoped for a different reaction from him.

"Well, don't feel the need to say anything more right now." She rubbed her gloved hands along her arms, more for comfort than warming. "Take time to assimilate. And while you're thinking, rest assured I intend to have this baby and take care of the child myself."

She pivoted away toward the house where she could salvage her pride, preferably in front of the fireplace, wrapped in her softest blanket with a warmed slice of cranberry-nut bread and a big glass of milk.

"Hey, hold on," he said, taking her arm gently. A thick, untamed lock of brown hair fell over his forehead. "Can we go inside together and talk about this some more?"

She should let him inside to talk, but her tender heart needed a break. Being alone inside the cabin felt too…intimate. Especially given the memories of making love there together in her brass bed. She settled for a compromise. "We can go around back to the sunroom."

Nodding, he motioned forward. "After you."

She sighed in relief. Bracing a hand on the logged exterior, she picked her way along the path running beside the cabin to the back of the home. She climbed the steps carefully, gripping the rail. She considered herself surefooted enough, especially after some rugged nature walks, but she needed to be all the more careful for her child. Nearly fainting while standing on an icy patch had reminded her that she needed to be more vigilant about her personal safety. At the door, she tapped in the security code and stepped inside.

The glassed-in space had been her haven this winter, a place to soak in nature without risking frostbite. For the holidays, she'd added a minitree and a string of snowflake lights.

She turned on the electric fireplace before claiming the rocking chair, leaving him the rustic futon and ensuring he couldn't sit beside her. She busied herself with unwinding her scarf, tugging off her gloves, and warming her hands in front of the artificial flames. Anything to distract herself from the outdoorsy scent of him filling her space.

Gil unzipped his parka before taking his seat. "I need for you to know I'm not upset. Just surprised."

"That's understandable." She clenched her fingers

into fists to keep from brushing aside that wayward lock of his hair.

"Of course I want to be a part of the child's life— my child's life. I'm here for support, and I don't just mean financially." He scrubbed a hand over his strong jaw. "I won't bail the way my birth father did to my birth mother."

She hadn't considered how this news might hit him, as the child of a single mom. Later, she would mull over the implications of those shadows in his eyes.

For now, though, she needed to focus on the present, on her baby. "Let's wait until later to speak about future plans. Right now is just about information. I would also ask that we not say anything to anyone else until I'm past my next doctor visit and the ultrasound."

He frowned. "Is there something wrong?"

"Not at all." Other than her autoimmune disease placing her into the high-risk category. But she absolutely did not want to delve into that discussion just yet. "I just prefer to wait until I have that ultrasound image and reassurance in hand."

"So you haven't even told your sisters?"

Hadn't she just said as much? She swallowed down a well of frustration, reminding herself how rocked she'd been by that first positive pregnancy test. "I wanted to tell you first. My sisters don't know. I thought we should make sure to tell your dad and my siblings on the same day so one doesn't feel slighted over being told second."

His broad shoulders relaxed, muscles rippling. "That's thoughtful of you. My dad will be over the moon. It'll give him something to obsess about while he's recovering from surgery."

At the mention of Lottie's surgery, a shiver of worry passed through her.

Gil pushed to his feet. "I should let you go inside before you get too cold. You need to take care of yourself."

His overprotective words made her bristle. She remembered well the sting of how her ex had reacted to her added health concerns. She snatched up her gloves and scarf before standing. "I'm fine, thank you."

"I'll be here in the morning to walk you over to your cookie exchange. It starts at ten, right? For brunch?"

"And crafts." She felt control of her world slipping away. "I can make my own way…"

He studied her for a handful of heartbeats before nodding. "If you wish. Although I'm leading a snowman-building competition in front of the lodge at the same time, so it's no trouble at all."

She could see the determination in his eyes. He would camp out on her porch if that's what it took. He intended to walk her over.

Might as well reassure him on this point and save her battles for the ones that mattered most. No doubt, there were plenty of decisions ahead of them. "Thanks for the offer, but my sisters will be walking with me, so there's no need to worry."

By noon the next day, Gil wasn't any closer to peace than the moment the baby bombshell had rocked his world. Throwing himself into his work wasn't helping the way it normally did. Still, he gave it his all as he pushed a snowball boulder for a group of women entering the snowman-building competition.

"Ladies, is this big enough now?" Straightening, Gil surveyed the seven icy globs dyed to look like skeins of yarn at the feet of their knitting-themed Mrs. Frosty.

The president of their group—the Purl Girls—raised her blue-mittened hand to her mouth and guffawed. "Does size matter? What do you think, friends?"

Purl Girl number three jabbed two sticks into the purple globe, knitting-needle style. "Depends on who you ask, right Veronica?"

Veronica—their fearless leader—winked at Gil. "That's just fine. I consider our masterpiece complete. Thank you for your help."

"Glad to be of assistance." Gil dusted the chunks of ice from his parka and walked past some snowy works of art—a pup on a doghouse, a five-foot-tall tiered wedding cake, a traditional snowman holding a hitchhiker sign requesting a lift to Florida. His favorite though? A family who'd figured out a way to build the tallest snowman using a smart technicality. They'd stacked the sections longways along the ground to create a sleeping yeti.

He suspected the honorable mention would go to the snow sculpture of a toilet—created by a mischievous group of teenage boys.

Gil climbed the steps to the metal dais, which happened to give him too perfect a view into the main lodge's picture window. The cookie exchange was in full swing beyond those panes of glass, where the mother of his child shared bags of treats with the other attendees. While the room was packed, Neve captivated his attention in her black leggings and a red plaid shirt that skimmed her knees.

She wound her way around tables filled with crafts in different stages of completion. Seeing those bird houses and wreaths brought back memories of the early days after his adoption, when his new mom had tried to bond with him over painting ornaments.

He'd struggled not to fidget and toppled the green paint, wrecking what little progress he'd managed on a macaroni-art decoration. He'd been sure his new family would give him back to the agency...

While now he understood how deeply the Hadleys loved him even then, he hated to think of his child feeling torn between homes. He couldn't figure out why Neve had brushed aside his offer to walk with her, a rejection that still stung. But he couldn't afford to press her, not when they already had co-parenting concerns to consider.

He drew in a breath of air so cold it threatened to freeze his nostrils closed and shifted his attention back to the competition. "Now that the construction is complete, we'll rope off the area so people can stroll by and cast votes. Categories will include, most original, tallest—" he glanced at the snoozing-yeti entry before continuing "—best traditional, and an honorable mention. The prize for each will be a one-hundred-dollar certificate to the ranch's gift shop and a professional photo shoot by our staff photographer."

"Wows" and cheers swelled from the crowd. Teens high-fived each other. A nearby little boy rambled his wish list to his parents. The Purl Girls tucked heads together, no doubt planning a yarn purchase from the gift shop's crafting corner.

Gil held up a hand for silence. "And that's not all. Finalists will be listed on our website with online voting for a grand prize winner."

Veronica shouted, "What's the prize for that?"

"Each vote will cost a dollar," Gil explained. "All of the money raised will be donated to a charity of the winner's choosing."

The clearing filled with thunderous applause, personifying that generous Top Dog spirit he appreciated. "Be sure not to miss our annual ugly-holiday-sweater party. This year, we're featuring a twist. We'll have a parade of dogs wearing the ugly creations."

As he made the announcement, he realized the irony of how he was the only employee without a pet. He'd told himself his long hours kept him from being a dog daddy, although one of his former girlfriends had insisted he lacked the ability to commit to another living being. That stung now more than it had then.

His gaze skated back to the picture window, drawn to the view of Neve holding up a picture frame which made him think about her thoughtful gift list. Personalized. Not generic like his pet-free, bachelor life. Did she have the same reservations about his ability to commit? If so, he was going to have to dispel them sooner rather than later.

Even if that meant pretending that he wasn't shaking in his boots at the thought of becoming a father.

Neve wondered if anyone else noticed she'd spent the past two hours pretending not to notice Gil hefting around giant snowballs in front of the lodge, flexing those muscles as he'd done with chopping firewood.

And she wasn't the only one who'd looked over at that window a few extra times as they'd painted their woodcrafts. The gifts lined a table, wet paint drying on toy trains, angels, dreidels, treetop stars, and her own smudged picture-frame ornament. Thank goodness she could salvage it by gluing some rose petals and baby's breath over the snafus.

A lump grew in her throat as she envisioned the piece with a photo of her child someday. What gifts would be in the stocking for her little one next year? Her fingers hovered over a hand-carved rattle painted pink. Nerves and excitement tangled up inside her as she tried to envision her little boy or girl. By Christmastime, her child might be past the stage of playing with rattles, learning to sit up. Embracing that first stage of independence.

As soon as the whimsical thoughts whispered through her mind, a more complicated thought chased after.

Would Gil want to come for the holidays, to see his child's first Christmas? She could envision that...

But what if he'd started a new relationship by then? Certainly that would be an issue at some future holiday. The future became trickier to navigate the more she thought about the years to come. Her mind kept creating flow charts of what could happen and each made her worry over a whole new path.

She rubbed her tight throat as she stared out the window at Gil helping a little boy add a block of packed snow to a small igloo.

Zelda leaned into her line of sight, placing a Santa Paws decoration to dry with the rest and be picked up the next day. "Love is in the air."

Neve looked toward her sister so fast her hip bumped the table, toppling a menorah. She set it upright again, thankful the gold paint hadn't smeared. "What do you mean?"

"Did you see the way River Jack and Priscilla were looking at each other last night?" Zelda waved a hand in front of her face. "Whew, they were simmering."

Neve gathered the extra dried flowers and deposited them into a bowl in the center for potpourri-making later. "She's going to be his nurse though."

"So they'll have even more time to get to know each other while he's recovering." Zelda waggled her eyebrows. "Maybe she could give him a sponge bath. Although now that I think that through further, changing bandages doesn't sound very romantic to me."

Neve froze, her sister's words calling to mind how

her ex had broken things off after her diagnosis. Was weakness a turn-off? She knew her sister hadn't meant it that way, but she couldn't help but think her former partner had viewed her illness as something that detracted from her appeal.

Before she'd found a medicine that helped to control her disease, she'd experience a lot of fatigue and achiness. It was better now, but she recalled the way those symptoms had made her feel—and the way her ex-boyfriend had reacted to last-minute changes in plans when she needed to rest.

Beside her, Isobel dropped her paintbrushes into a jar, unaware of Neve's dark thoughts. Isobel transferred her star to dry with the rest. "Maybe she'll wipe his brow and sit beside his bed, reading out loud to him."

Zelda tapped her chin. "What would she read? I don't see River Jack going for Jane Austen."

"I'm sure she could find something he would like." Isobel huffed in exasperation. "You need more romance in your soul."

Zelda winked. "Troy doesn't have any complaints."

Her sisters' talk of love and romance had Neve cringing inside all the more. They were so happy, so settled. And while she didn't begrudge them their happiness...

Isobel reached for her canvas sack. "Well, I need to pick up Lottie for her doctor's appointment. Cash hung out with her this morning so I could enjoy some sister time, but he needs to head into work this afternoon."

Neve rested a hand on Isobel's wrist. "Please text me how it goes."

"Absolutely," Isobel said.

While she'd thought she grasped her sister's worry before, her own maternal instincts already churned inside her, bringing a new level of understanding. Neve fretted over every bite she ate, her rest, vitamins.

And of course, what if her child had inherited the gene for the same disease that had caught Neve unaware? Or Lottie's spina bifida? She'd included the information when filling out the paperwork at the obstetrician's office. He'd taken note and assured her the proper screening would occur.

The likelihood of passing on lupus was small, but present. And a possibility she should share with Gil before her appointment. If he opted to join her—and she would offer—she didn't want him to be blindsided.

Her hand pressed to her stomach protectively. She already loved her child so deeply. She just hoped she could be as good of a mother as Isobel.

Isobel hitched her bag onto her shoulder, a Cocoa the Caring Canine logo on the sack. "I'm praying we don't have any more delays. River Jack and Lottie are limiting their gatherings to outdoors or small groups, just to be on the safe side. We can't risk any last-minute infections."

Zelda slid her arms into her parka and flipped her

braid free. "What do you say I come with you? I know how you hate to drive in the mountains, although that makes this a curious place to live."

"Thank you," Isobel said. "I won't turn down a chauffeur offer."

"Hold on." Neve grabbed her overcoat. "I'll come along too."

She followed her siblings as they moved from the craft area into the soaring entryway. With luck, she could make it past Gil and delay their next conversation just a bit longer, until her nerves had settled and she had those mental flowcharts under control.

Neve tugged on her mittens just as a blast of cold air whipped through the open door. "Maybe we can have supper together afterward."

Isobel smiled her gratitude. "You're both too thoughtful."

Wincing, Neve felt a pinch of guilt over using her sisters to avoid Gil. Not that she let it stop her from sidling past the porch rockers and down the salted stairs while Gil placed signs in front of each snowy entrant with numbers and the entrant's last name.

She was almost in the clear. A few more steps, then she and her sisters would be blocked from view by the cluster of ladies she'd seen at the knitting circle earlier in the week.

Neve glanced back over her shoulder for one more glimpse of Gil—

A high-pitched bark carried from the forest a moment before a beagle puppy bounded clear of the tree line. Ears flopping, the tiny hound raced past her, heading straight toward Gil standing beside a towering snowman.

Chapter Five

Gil panicked. And he wasn't a guy who lost his cool easily.

But a strange puppy was dodging and weaving around the hands trying to grasp him—or her—and was now making a beeline toward Neve. With the memory of her passing out still fresh in his mind, he worried about her slipping on the ice. Sure, she was standing still. For now.

He bolted toward her, half running, half skating his boots along the slicker patches. The beagle darted around Frosty, then jumped over the lounging, tallest snowman. Just inches away from capture, Gil extended his arm. Only to have the little escape artist shoot between the legs of a Purl Girl.

Squeals and shouts from the crowd spurred the dog on until it plowed right into the doghouse exhibit, pausing long enough to shake away snow, ears flapping.

A sharp whistle pierced the mayhem and Gil pivoted quickly. Neve had her fingers between her lips, letting loose another whistle.

She lowered her arm to her side as the crowd quieted. "Everyone, please don't move. I've got this."

Carefully, she knelt. She extended her hand, otherwise completely still. The beagle baby swiveled to look where all other eyes were focused.

At Neve.

Pretty as you please, the puppy pranced over to her, sniffed her hand, twice, then wagged its tail so hard the dog's whole body followed suit. Neve scooped the pup into her arms and stood, getting plenty of doggy kisses on her chin. "Hello, little one. Where are your people? Aren't you a cute—" she dipped her head slightly "—cute fellow."

Gil tugged his zipper back up, the jacket having come loose during his sprint to rescue a damsel who apparently didn't need his help. "Who knew you're a dog whisperer?"

"He was only reflecting the energy of everyone around him," she said as some of the guests repaired their snowman entrants, while others departed for different activities. "Once I had his attention, he mirrored my calm."

That made sense. Although tough to achieve in the heat of the moment. Gil tugged off a glove and reached for his phone. "I guess we should let Hollie and Jacob know there's a loose animal with no tags on the property."

"Good idea. They can check the guest sign-ins. And while they're doing that, I'll take the puppy to the veterinarian's office so they can scan for a microchip." She stroked along the pup's spine in a slow, rhythmic way that soon had him snuggling nearer.

Gil envied that beagle.

"Do what, now?" he said, his brain scrambled by her closeness. No surprise. "You're going into town? With the puppy? What if he climbs all over you in the car?"

"Fair point," she conceded. "I'll ask my sister if there's an extra kennel at the grooming salon."

Not a chance. Neve had been dodging him for hours, and this was his chance to get some answers. "I'll drive you and we can finally have that conversation you've been avoiding."

She opened and closed her mouth as if to argue, then surrendered with a nod.

"Good," he said. "That's settled, then. I'll carry this little fellow so you don't slip, and you can text Jacob and Hollie."

Her chin jutted stubbornly as if she might argue. The pup whimpered and the irritation melted off her face, replaced by concern. "I need a quick word with my sisters, then let's get moving."

Given the set brace of her delicate shoulders, he got the distinct impression she still wasn't ready to talk about plans for the future. For their child. If he pushed her, she might well shut him down all over again. No question, he would need to finesse the conversation. Probably best to keep the talk light until he saw an opening.

However, make no mistake. She may have delayed

the discussion a little longer, but they still had a boatload to work through and he hadn't forgotten. Not by a long shot.

Thirty minutes and a few miles later, Neve scrolled through her text messages, the beagle puppy in a carrier on the floor of Gil's truck. The heater blasted a welcome warmth, the temperature outside dropping. Her plan to keep Gil at arm's length until the dust settled about their baby news had gone awry. When he'd offered to drive her...

Well, she had struggled to resist this man long before today, so it was no surprise she'd given in to ride along.

She tucked away her cell phone. "Hollie says they don't have a guest registered who noted bringing a beagle, but she'll call around to check. Sometimes people don't declare their pet in order to avoid a deposit."

"That sure doesn't help if their dog goes missing without a collar." He kept both hands on the steering wheel, navigating the twisty mountain roads with care. Icy branches glistened in the mid-afternoon sun. "Let's hope he has a microchip."

"He hasn't been neutered yet, and often, that's when the microchip gets placed. There's still a possibility though. An animal doesn't have to be under anesthesia for a chip to be inserted. It's just a little pinch."

She leaned down to the kennel and wriggled her

fingers through the front grate. The pup nosed her and she gave him a little stroke of comfort, but a quick peek assured her he was out for the count. Probably exhausted after all the excitement. He'd eaten the canned puppy food and lapped up some water before nestling into the cozy fleece blanket in the crate.

"You're great with animals." Gil paused at a stop sign, waiting while a VW with a wreath on the grill inched up the hill and turned. "Why don't you have a dog—or a cat? Or am I mistaken?"

He accelerated, jostling over a pothole, the gear in his back bench seat rattling. Snowshoes. A helmet. Some kind of cold-weather survival kit. The man was prepared for anything.

"You're correct. I don't have a pet right now, but I get my snuggles in with my sisters' dogs, without the veterinarian bills. Of course Cocoa is working most of the time, but Zelda's little Maisie is a cuddler." She twisted in her seat to look at him, allowing herself an unguarded moment to study the handsome lines of his face. His strong jaw and cheekbones. His good looks such a mix of rugged and classical. "Did you know that precious pup was abandoned in a shelter? She belonged to an elderly lady, and when she had to go to a care home, the adult kids just dumped Maisie."

"That's so sad," he said shaking his head. "I'm glad she landed well. But you still haven't answered my question about why you don't have a pet of your own. You're a wildlife biologist after all."

"Fair point. While I was in school and working, it

didn't seem practical. Now that I've finished my PhD, that clears some of my schedule. Although my time will fill soon enough with the baby."

A tic started in the corner of his eye, but he stayed quiet. She knew they needed to talk about concrete plans for the baby soon, but she just wasn't ready. She'd already had two such massive life changes in the past year, first with her lupus diagnosis and now with the pregnancy.

But she recognized Gil needed something from her, some indication of how they would venture through the future.

She took a breath and told herself not to stress about it. Worrying wasn't good for her or their child. Instead, she opted to keep the conversation flowing, even if it wasn't superserious.

She tapped his elbow lightly. "Ham or turkey?"

"Pardon me?" Frowning, he turned on the blinker, a mistletoe air freshener on the rearview mirror swaying.

"For the holidays," she explained. "Do you prefer ham or turkey?"

"Turkey, smoked. By me." He hummed as if already appreciating the taste. "I stay up all night long watching over it."

"In the cold. I should have known," she said with a laugh. "I'm fine with either one, in case you were wondering."

"You're jumping ahead there." He angled his head toward her, eyes still fixed on the road, sludge on the sides. "Give me a second to catch up with the game. Gingerbread or sugar cookies?"

"Gingerbread." Her mouth watered and her stomach rumbled. "Still warm from the oven, served with whipped cream."

"Whipped cream?" He winked. "I have ideas for what to do with the leftovers."

"Rein it in, cowboy."

"Yes, ma'am," he said with a nod, a light brown lock sliding over his forehead. "I bet you save and reuse gift bags. No offense meant."

"None taken. Gran taught me to be thrifty. And she also taught me to care deeply for the environment." Memories scrolled of taking nature walks because they were free and picking up trash along the way. She thought of learning to clip coupons with her sisters at her grandmother's table and scanning the sales paper for deals. And yet at the reading of her will, they'd learned she'd left behind a tidy sum for each of them. "I may have even ironed out tissue paper during financially leaner days in college."

His mother would have liked her. Both moms, actually. The thought knocked the air out of him for a moment. "Your turn with the questions."

"No questions, really. I was, uh, trying to see what your holidays are like, thinking ahead to what traditions you'll be sharing with the baby." She chewed her lip for a moment, eyes drawn to a family draping lights on a fir outside their cabin.

His throat moved in a low swallow. "This time next year, we'll be buying Christmas presents for our kid."

The weight of that made her jittery, so she defaulted to humor, much easier than facing heavier emotions. "Just so you're not buying a dirt bike for an infant."

"Heard and understood. Regardless of what you may think, I take the safety of others very seriously." There was no missing the sincerity in his voice, along with a hint of defensiveness. "For what it's worth, stores carry perfectly safe little sleds for babies."

"We can negotiate." She was thinking more along the lines of hiking with the baby in a backpack, teaching her child the names of all the trees and birds. "What was your favorite Christmas gift you ever received from Santa?"

She settled into the comfort of the questions and reminiscing. It was nice to be around him without having her insides in a turmoil.

A smile kicked up the corner of his mouth. "A Nintendo Wii, the year it debuted. Remember how it had the controllers where you had to move around?" He glanced at her and when she shook her head, he chuckled. "Well, anyway, I loved that. You may have guessed that I've always preferred to stay active."

"I've noticed," she said with a laugh.

"What about you?" He powered the truck from the back road to a smoother two-lane route that led into Moonlight Ridge. "Favorite gift?"

"A metal detector," she answered quickly, which

was odd, because until this moment, she'd forgotten all about it.

"For real?" His eyebrows lifted in surprise. "How old were you?"

"Ten." Her gaze skittered away from the quaint little town and back toward the heavily forested mountain. "I loved to walk in the woods even then, so my folks figured maybe I could make some money in the process."

"Did it work?" He stopped at Main Street's one traffic light.

"At first, I just found the occasional pocket change." Her mind filled with the echo of wind in the trees from long ago, of the peaceful solitude. Nature's sounds serenading her soul. As if life was preparing her for the way she needed to guard her physical and emotional reserves later in life because of her autoimmune disease. "But this one time, I found a college class ring and we were able to trace the owner. I got a twenty-dollar reward."

"That's a cool story."

She rolled her eyes. "The kids at school told me I was stupid not to sell it for gold. I bought a bag of birdseed and went on a hike to feed the wildlife."

Slowing, he turned into the emergency vet's parking lot. Dog bone–shaped lights were draped around the doorway where clients walked in and out with carriers and pets on leashes. "But you were a good girl, even then."

"I played by the rules. I still do, I guess." She avoided his gaze by picking up the small dog crate.

"So how did you end up having a fling with the ultimate rule breaker?" He shifted into Park, the truck idling. "That's me, in case I wasn't clear."

"I got your meaning." And as much as she wanted to run, he deserved an honest answer. "I wish I had an answer for you on that one. That would make this a lot easier."

Armed with enough puppy gear for a whole litter, Gil tucked the small kennel in the back seat this time to give Neve more leg room. She had to be exhausted after the long day at the ranch and then hours in the emergency vet clinic. The sun had already dipped below the horizon. The puppy had been vaccinated, fed, and given a short potty walk before loading up.

"Are you warm enough?" he called over the seat, resisting the urge to sweep her glossy dark hair over and press a kiss to her neck.

"All good," she assured him. "It's still warm from when you ran to fill up the truck and get supper while the receptionist printed the paperwork. It all smells amazing, by the way, and I am starving."

A sack of burgers, fries, fruit cups, milk, and water bottles all waited on the front seat. "I wasn't sure what you wanted, so I ordered a bit of everything. Well, actually, a lot of everything because I'm more than a little hungry myself."

"You drive and I'll unwrap everything." She pulled

two burgers from the bag while he cranked the engine again. "I'll pay you back for the vet bill if you'll tell me your Venmo details."

"My treat." He opened his Spotify and selected holiday tunes to play softly.

"We can discuss it later." She passed his burger and napkins, the scent of fresh-broiled meat teasing the air and his tastebuds.

He took the food and ignored her discussion about money. He didn't want to wreck a surprisingly easygoing outing with an argument. "It's a shame he didn't have a microchip."

About halfway through the exam, he started to worry the cute little fellow might be ill. The veterinarian had asked questions about previous vaccinations, then did a parvo test to make sure the deadly disease wasn't lurking. Now the pup had preventives on board.

Outside his pickup, more traffic filled the road than when they'd come down the mountain earlier. Cars filled with people headed home from school and work. A few others had Christmas trees strapped to their vehicles' roofs, taillights glowing.

Neve draped a napkin over her lap and fished out two fat fries, her toes tapping along to "Jingle Bells."

"Still no luck finding an owner. Hollie says she's texted every guest and called the local shelter and veterinary offices."

"How could someone just let this defenseless creature wander off without searching for him?" His eyes darted to the rearview mirror to check on their passenger. Gil had positioned the kennel so he could see inside the front grate. The puppy's belly rose and fell with deep sleep. The dark truck cab seemed to have settled him all the more.

"Hollie did mention one of the vets had a mama-dog client—a beagle—that delivered about eight weeks ago. He implied the owners may have released the puppy at the ranch when they couldn't find a home."

His jaw clenched in frustration. "It's happened before. I even found a box of kittens left in the canoe shed last spring. Luckily, a couple of the staff members were on the lookout for a new pet. Doc Barnett adopted another for his grandkids. And the two wilder ones of the bunch are now barn cats."

"Lucky for that litter, but holy cow, eventually you'll run out of people on staff to take them if animals keep getting dumped. That really breaks my heart."

"Mine too." It appeared that while he and Neve were different in so many ways, they were united in their love of animals. And cheeseburgers. "But let's focus on this puppy. We should come up with something to call him, just until he's settled in a home."

She chewed through a couple more fries pensively. "What about names that tie into nature? Our first sight of him was barreling out of the woods, after all."

Intriguing, and fitting, given Neve's career. "That could work. What are you thinking about for possible choices?"

She chugged a gulp of milk before pulling out her phone to google. "How about something like Huckleberry, Griffin, Barley, Rocky, Heath…"

"Bear or Moose?"

She scrunched her nose playfully as they cleared the town limits. "He doesn't look much like a moose."

"Fair enough." He raised an eyebrow. "What about Puddles? That's water themed and he sure left enough of them on the vet's exam table."

She frowned playfully as they turned off the highway. "Or Oakley."

"Cute. Let's put that one in the maybe column. But not quite there yet…" Icicle lights glowed along a cabin roofline as they drove along the narrow mountain road back up the mountain. "What about a holiday-themed name, in honor of the time of year?"

"Hmm, that has potential." She pointed toward a rooftop with a plastic Santa and sleigh. "Rudolph. And we could call him Rudy."

We?

He liked the sound of that even more than he liked the name. And the name was a real winner, a sentiment that seemed echoed by the sound system cuing up music about that special red-nosed reindeer. "Rudy it is."

She tapped her container of milk against his bottled water. "Cheers."

He gulped a swallow to seal the deal. How much longer would the goodwill between them last? How far could he press her to have that talk? "When we get back to your place, I'll unload all the supplies from the veterinarian's office. Lucky he was well stocked so we didn't have to go to the store."

"I thought this would be your weekend with Rudy, joint custody and all." She bit off a large bite of her burger.

He glanced over at her quickly, only to find a playful smile on her lips. "You got me there, for a second."

After chewing, she continued, "Of course I'm keeping the puppy—until we find him a home. I'm the one who's home more, which makes for far smoother house-training."

And just that fast, she'd booted him out of Rudy's life. While he understood her reasoning on that one, he intended to make sure she didn't eject him from his child's life as well. "So, we've been dodging around discussing plans for the baby all day." He held up a hand, a plan forming in his mind for how to make the inevitable conversation easier. "Hear me out. You'd mentioned wanting to wait to tell anyone about the pregnancy until after your ultrasound. Why don't we wait to make any plans until then too. Let's just use this time to iron out getting along together."

If they were going to co-parent, they at least needed to understand one another better. They couldn't spend the next eighteen years trying to find the right time to bring up a tricky topic of discussion. It seemed important to get a better handle on each other so they could be good parents. Good partners, even if they weren't together. Their child deserved no less.

"What exactly do you mean?" she asked suspiciously. "You have to know sex would only complicate things."

"I agree."

"You do?" Her eyes went wide with shock.

He would have laughed at the surprise in her voice if there hadn't been so much at stake. "That's not what I'm suggesting." Even though he would give just about anything to be invited back into her bed. Anything except risk the chance to establish a more lasting connection for the sake of their child. "I'm merely saying we should hang out, get to know each other better, because heaven knows, we didn't spend a whole lot of time talking before."

And just that fast, the heat of the chemistry sparked in the air, like static connecting them. Memories of their end-of-summer fling filled his mind and his senses, making him ache to be with her again. Had he pushed her too far this evening? Had he missed an important window with her? Rather than risk saying the wrong thing, he waited. If nothing else, he understood her more measured way of life, her need to think things through.

Finally, she wadded up her empty wrapper and nodded. "Okay, let's give it a try. There are certainly plenty of activities around the ranch to keep ourselves occupied. Especially around the holidays."

A sigh of relief shuddered through him, along with a swell of victory, greater than sky diving.

Chapter Six

Neve hadn't been this nervous about a date since... Well, she couldn't remember when. Of course she'd never really "dated" Gil. They'd launched headlong into a fling, one unwise on a number of levels, so she'd kept the relationship a secret, even from her sisters.

Her hand slid to the small, almost unnoticeable bump where her child rested. Could she really look at their brief affair as unwise when it had brought her this baby?

Except she needed to remember this wasn't a real date. Just a series of outings to find their path to friendship. She winced at the word. Too benign a label for her complex feelings for the father of her child.

A man currently looking way too hot as he stood beside an old-fashioned sleigh parked in front of her cabin.

A Belgian draft horse pawed at the snow, hitched to the shiny red vehicle. Snowflakes fell at a slow, snow-globe pace, lazily dancing to the ground, the snowfall this year still setting records.

With a sweep of his arm, Gil bowed. "Your chariot awaits, my lady."

Moonlight streamed over him, showcasing the handsome planes of his face with his beard-stubbled jaw. Holding the horse's bridle, he had a timeless air in his jeans and a sherpa jacket with the collar turned up. But then, he'd always worn an untamed vibe, like an explorer trekking through the unknown as if that wasn't a scary or downright terrifying thing to do.

She shook off the fanciful notion and picked her way down the shoveled walk, her stomach churning with butterflies. "What a fun surprise." She flipped her scarf around her neck and tugged on her gloves. "When you said to dress warmly for the caroling, I thought we would be walking."

Her breath huffed white clouds into the air.

"Only the best for you," he said with a roguish grin. "I also thought we would have more privacy to talk this way. The paths will be packed with carolers."

The annual event at the ranch was one of the few open to the residents of Moonlight Ridge. Many of the attendees and staff dressed in vintage costumes, like a throwback to a Dickens era. Already, strains of "Greensleeves" drifted on the chilly breeze.

She extended a hand, her pulse speeding. "Would you like to help me up?"

He bypassed her hand and clasped her waist, lifting. "I sure would."

Squealing, she rested her fingers on his broad shoulders as he swooped her up. His muscles rippled against her and his strength stirred her almost as much as his smile.

The sleigh dipped ever so slightly as she settled into the cushioned bench and placed her canvas sack on the floorboards. "Rudy sends his best."

Gil swung up into the seat beside her and clasped the reins, launching the sleigh into motion. Bells chimed on the draft horse with each step, the runners cutting through the snow with a soft swish. "How's our little puppy fellow doing today? Any ill effects from the vaccination or adjusting to his new home with you?"

"When I left, he was all tuckered out from a bath at the grooming salon. He was snoring in his kennel after a big dinner and a run in the yard."

He chuckled. "I tried to make it downtown to get him some toys, but work ran long. The stables needed extra help brushing down the horses. While I was there, I learned of a last-minute cancellation for the sleigh. And here I am."

And here they were.

Gliding over the hilly mounds toward the main lodge, the jingle bells lifted her spirts, making her think that it sure was a romantic evening for an event she didn't want to call a date.

She soaked in the sight of holiday cheer, the path illuminated by flowing red strips. "I can't think of a year I've been more in the Christmas spirit."

"I brought hot cocoa and extra blankets to keep us warm. Just say the word."

His thoughtfulness touched her. But then he'd always been kind that way. Even during the days of their secret fling, she'd woken up some mornings to muffins on her kitchen table, flowers on her pillow, hot coffee in an insulated mug on her bedside table.

As his gaze was glued to the path ahead, she took in his silhouette. Thinking about how many times she'd run her fingers along his bristly jaw. She'd always been attracted to him, but thinking about all the ways he'd made her feel special, even when it wasn't serious, stirred something inside her chest. "Thank you for arranging all of this."

"It's easier to make an evening like this happen when we're living in a back-to-nature resort."

A cluster of teens jogged past, haphazardly slipping along the path as they clutched one another and giggled. The Purl Girls strolled at a slower pace, humming "Away in the Manger" as they made their way toward the main lodge.

"This is perfect." She shoulder-bumped him, his aftershave spicy and enticing. "Thank you."

"If you get tired, let me know." He tugged a wool blanket from under the bench with one hand, the other still clasping the reins. "I was reading online, in an article about pregnancy, that you may need more sleep."

Defensiveness whispered to life inside her as she took the afghan and draped it over her knees. "Please know that I'm not going to break. My doctor and I can manage my health."

She'd battled her emotions when it came to her

health, knowing she needed to care for herself but wrestling with the idea that she had to respect new limitations. It hadn't been easy to readjust her view of herself as strong when there were things she couldn't—or shouldn't—do anymore.

"Will you speak up, though, if you need something?" He glanced at her, eyes narrowed. "I understand why you're focused on your niece right now, but you need to think of yourself."

Tension tightened her shoulders and she couldn't stop herself from snapping back defensively. "You're one to speak about asking for help, Mr. Free Spirit."

He held up a gloved hand. "I apologize. The last thing I want is to ruin this night when I've been looking forward to seeing you all day."

"I'm sorry too." She adjusted the blanket over her knees, covering her boots for good measure. A sweet warmth spread through her. "I didn't mean to be prickly."

"Better that we iron all of that out now, before the baby arrives."

Easier said than done. At least they were both determined to try.

She reached into her canvas bag for her cell phone and a slip of paper she'd picked up at the lodge during lunch. "In the interest of learning more about each other... I brought one of the Getting to Know You bingo cards from the ranch's games gathering."

"Ah, you planned ahead."

"It's the scholar in me. I never showed up for school

without my homework." She took comfort in planning ahead. Meeting Gil had been a great big, unexpected curve ball. She clicked on her cell phone light and shone it over the printed paper. "So, let's start with... What's your dream job?"

"I already have it," he said without hesitation. "What about you?"

"Department chair. Or dean," she said primly. It might not sound exciting to him, but to her? It was the mountaintop. She moved on to the next question. "Have you been to another country?"

He steered the horse to a less-populated path, one that would eventually lead to the lodge, but with less traffic. And more privacy.

"Of course. Quite a few, actually." The sleigh jostled along the trail and he stretched an arm along the seat behind her, cupping her shoulder. "I used to work for a travel adventure company. I've been ziplining in Costa Rica. Deep-sea diving in the Galapagos Islands. Snow skiing in France."

"Wow, that sounds exciting." And a little scary. She adjusted her phone light over the card and read, "'What made you accept your current job?'"

"To be near my dad, of course." Gil said, his affection for his father apparent. "What about you? Do you like to travel? Although I'm guessing if you went to the Galapagos Islands, you would be on the beach reading a book—looking incredibly sexy in a bikini."

Her mouth twitched with a laugh, while also realizing such exotic locations and adventurous activities had never been on her wish list.

"I spent a year in Canada on a research project for conservation and wildlife biology." A magical time of reflection and intellectual stimulation. Her grandmother had said she was carrying the wonder of the Tennessee mountains with her into a career. "I had the most amazing opportunities to commune with nature."

"So we both love the outdoors. That's something we have in common."

True. But… "Although you have to admit we experience the outdoors in very different ways."

"Fair enough." He nodded. "Pass me that bingo card."

"Sure, you can have a turn." She handed him the slip of paper.

He took it from her hand and passed her the reins. Then tore the card into pieces. He stuffed them into his pocket and clasped the reins again. "Sounds like we've both lived a lot of life already. I want to put a new spin on this game. Let's create a Couples Bucket List."

"That sounds fun," she said, surprised. "Where did you come up with that idea?"

He grinned, crinkles fanning from his eyes. "I looked up conversation starters on the internet."

"You did your homework too." She clapped her hands in delight. "Now, that's how to impress the teacher. What suggestions did you find in that search?"

"Things like take a cooking class together. Go to a yoga retreat. Make a relationship time capsule." He paused, frowning. "Complete a puzzle."

Laughing, she covered her mouth. "You don't sound enthusiastic about that last one."

His cheeks puffed with a long exhale. "That's a lot of sitting still."

She couldn't hold back another giggle at his self-deprecating humor. When he grinned in return, her heart stuttered. The jingle bells chimed in the silence between them, and he angled closer, hesitating, waiting. She swayed toward him and their lips grazed. Holding briefly, until they settled back into their seats just as the lodge came into view, along with a few too many curious eyes for them to continue.

Without a doubt, sifting through her feelings for Gil was going to be far more complicated than could be handled by any bingo questionnaire. And the stakes were far higher than any game.

When planning their next outing, Gil made sure there was less chance for interruption. Moonlight Ridge's fancy new pet-supply store was packed, but not with folks from the ranch. Townspeople browsed, some with dogs on a leash sniffing the displays. A handful of children stood at the fish tanks with their noses pressed against the glass.

He strolled alongside Neve down the aisle of puppy sweaters and costumes. Rudy rested in the shopping cart on a new plaid bed. She'd argued that the ranch had plenty of pet paraphernalia there for the asking, but he'd insisted that he wanted Rudy to have things of his own to take to his new home when he left.

At the sheen of tears in her eyes, he could already see the affection in her eyes and suspected she might be considering keeping him.

Now, as he eyed a chew toy shaped like a candy cane, he couldn't help but think about someday shopping for their child. Buying clothes and teethers.

He moved from the chewy items to tap a spinning magazine tower filled with how-to periodicals about pet care. Maybe he should expand his reading beyond pregnancy articles online and pick up a couple of parenting books.

"He's a cute little fella. I'd always heard puppies could be full of energy—and puddles—but he seems pretty easy," he said. "Any word about possible placements for him?"

"The veterinarian's office and the local shelter didn't have any new suggestions when I called again today." She wriggled a stuffed Santa toy in front of Rudy and squeezed the squeaker in the belly. The puppy tugged at the toy boot until Neve surrendered his gift. "The receptionists assured me they have my phone number. I got the feeling they already have too many strays who don't have a warm home to hang out in."

"Do you want to keep Rudy?" He had to admit, he wouldn't mind seeing the little guy grow up.

"My sisters each have a dog. I've always wanted

one. I worry, though, that I might be taking on too much with a baby on the way." Her forehead furrowed and she pushed the cart around a corner into a row of dog food. "I need to be fair to this little one."

He scratched along the twinge in his heart. "I'm sure he won't have trouble finding a home, especially since he will have been vetted."

She wove around a family of five studying different dog bowls. "Did you have pets growing up?"

He shook his head. "My bio mom didn't have the money and my adoptive mom was very allergic."

"What about now?" she asked chewing her bottom lip. "Maybe Rudy could be your puppy."

If she wasn't interested in keeping the pup, then he had to admit to being tempted. Maybe his dad could help out with dog walking once he recovered. "Then you wouldn't have to say goodbye since you would see him whenever I see our child."

"I wasn't trying to pressure you." She rested a hand on his arm. "I promise."

Her touch warm through his flannel, he took in the sight of her in slim-fit jeans, a creamy-white sweater and a plaid scarf looped around her neck that made him ache to grasp the ends and tug her closer.

He tipped his head to work the crick out of his neck. "Let's see if the owner steps up after all before worrying about hypotheticals."

"Fair enough." She shifted to grasp the cart with both hands, turning worried eyes toward the puppy. "I just want him to have the very best home."

"Of course you do." He placed a palm low on her back, a host of memories flooding in of a time when they would have taken those touches all the way to the bedroom. "You have a soft spot for animals. I could tell that by the way you studied birds and other woodland creatures during our walks."

Her mouth curved in a nostalgic smile. "I would sit in a treehouse all day, reading books and cataloguing birds, if I could—"

Someone jostled him from behind, cutting the moment short. He pivoted protectively to find a teenager cradling a chihuahua against her Moonlight Ridge Community College sweatshirt.

"Excuse me," the girl said, adjusting her hold on the little yipper in an elf sweater. "Which toy do you recommend? I'm pet sitting my granny's dog while she's in the hospital and I would like to get little Bella something useful so I can send Granny a bunch of selfies with Bella."

Neve pulled away from Gil self-consciously, reaching over the canned food for a Nylabone. "One of my sisters has a tiny dog and she loves these bones right here."

"What about that poofy puppy purse over there?"

"Cuter than the bone, sure. But I'll bet the stuffed toy gets shredded down to the squeaker in no time flat."

"Oh wow. Thanks." She glanced back over her shoulder. "You two sure are a cute couple. Good luck with your baby."

"What?" Gil jolted, exchanging a shocked look with Neve. The baby? How did this girl know?

The girl's hand drifted to pet Rudy. "Your baby. He's a cutie-pie."

A sigh shuddered through Neve and she laughed softly. "He sure is."

And as Gil watched Neve adjust the bright new dog collar, he couldn't deny the shift in his chest, right around the part of him that shied away from any kind of commitment. Rudy didn't have to worry about a home if no one claimed the puppy, because Gil intended to keep him.

The next day, Neve still wasn't sure why she felt betrayed by Gil's request to keep Rudy if no one claimed him. Maybe worry about Lottie's surgery coming up in three days had her on edge.

She probably should have bowed out of her plans with Gil for the evening, but the clock was ticking on spending time together without the pressure of questions about the baby and their future. So she stood at her gate waiting for him to arrive while Rudy ran zoomies around her little fenced yard.

They'd originally planned to attend an Enchanted Forest party over at Ian Greer's neighboring tree farm, but the weatherperson forecasted rain, so the event had been rescheduled. So they'd shifted plans at the last minute to watch movies at her place. Selecting shows had been a revelation in and of itself, finding the sweet spot between a shoot-em-up action flick and a tearjerker romance film.

She heard the sound of cars rumbling along the road and her heart pounded faster until she realized it was just her sisters coming home to their two cabins, beside hers. Once upon a time, she and her sisters had dreamed of living this close together. The past few months had been wonderful, popping over for a cup of coffee anytime. Hanging out on the porch late at night to watch fireflies light the night sky, then later, watch the autumn leaves fall.

But their time of closeness was drawing to an end. Soon Zelda would marry Troy, moving in with him and his daughter Harper. Isobel, Cash, and Lottie would stay in their place, thanks to Cash's job at the ranch. Neve, however, would be heading home soon, her sabbatical over and her funds from Gran for the Moonlight Ridge trip running dry. She swallowed down a lump of emotion.

Zelda's little VW bug pulled up in front of her cabin at the same time Isobel's van parked beside Cash's truck.

The wheelchair ramp lowered on the side of the minivan and Lottie waved. "Hey, Aunt Neve."

"Hello, kiddo," Neve hollered back, clipping a leash to Rudy's collar before walking through the gate toward her sisters.

Her sisters didn't know about her evening plans, but they would soon enough if Gil arrived before they got inside. She took her time as the puppy bounded to the side and back again, taking the steps twice in his enthusiasm.

Zelda circled to the minivan's back hatch as it swooped open, and pulled out a bag. "Wow, Isobel, you and Lottie sure cleared out the store while I was at work."

Isobel shrugged, not looking in the least embarrassed. "Lottie and I did some online shopping for a pickup order of everything she wants to keep her occupied during recovery."

Neve started to ask why they hadn't gone inside to choose, then remembered her sister talking about limiting exposure to other people as much as possible this near the surgery date. A van load full of toys and crafts seemed precious little to give a kid facing major surgery at Christmastime.

"Yeah," Lottie said as her wheelchair cleared the ramp. "I wanted to go on a car ride, so that's why we didn't just get it all from the delivery man."

Zelda peeked into the bag in her arms. "Do I spy a new tablet in there?"

"You betcha." Lottie looked back over her shoulder. "Mom, can I play with the puppy? Please, pretty please?"

Isobel tugged her daughter's pink hood up before returning to the van to begin unhooking Cocoa from her car harness. "Sweetie, it looks like your aunt has plans. She's all dressed up."

"Aunt Neve, are you going someplace? I could watch the puppy."

Neve tugged at her red jacket self-consciously. She couldn't deny she'd taken far more care with her appearance than was warranted for an evening in. "My friend Gil and I are just going to have a movie night."

Lottie's eyes went wide. "I like movies. Wanna have a movie night with us? My mom has the very best snacks."

Neve glanced at her sister, wondering if she should keep her distance. "I wouldn't want to risk us bringing germs…"

Isobel smiled. "It's totally up to your aunt and her *friend*. Since Gil's been around his dad, we're somewhat in the same circle of germ avoidance."

Biting her lip, Neve struggled with how to respond. What would Gil say? Would he be upset with her for changing plans? She felt torn.

Regardless, after their kiss earlier that week, a part of her knew it would be safer to stay in a group. "Of course we would like to join you, Lottie."

"With the puppy?" her niece pleaded. "Please, Mommy?"

Isobel glanced over from the open van door where she was hooking a leash to the chocolate Labrador Retriever's collar. "You know the rules before Cocoa can have playdates. We have to be careful that Cocoa's friends are healthy. If she gets sick, then she won't be able to help you until she's well. What do you need to ask Aunt Neve?"

Lottie nodded. "Did Rudy get his medicine shots and a checkup? Is he sick or anything?"

Neve admired how her sister had helped Lottie advocate for her dog. The two had such a beautiful partnership. "Rudy has had all his vaccines and he's superhealthy. But he's also had a really long day and puppies sleep a lot. Maybe they can play another day? For now, how about I hold him for you to pet before he goes to take a nap?"

She scooped up Rudy, cradling his legs close to her so he felt secure. Angling toward her niece, she smiled as Lottie carefully stroked two fingers along the puppy's back, then rubbed his floppy ear.

Lottie giggled. "His ears are silkier than Cocoa's. Are you gonna keep him? I hope so, because Cocoa would really enjoy a friend. Maisie's sweet and all, but she's tiny. She also naps a lot. Cocoa has to have playtime too."

As her niece continued to pet the pup, Neve realized that her child would likely grow up with this dog. Her throat went tight and tears welled in her eyes. She knew Gil wanted to keep Rudy, but right now, so did she. If she felt this conflicted over sharing a puppy they'd only just met, how would she ever manage splitting time spent with their child?

"Aunt Neve," Lottie said, her hood sliding back again to reveal her pigtails. "Is Mr. Gil your *boy-friend*?"

Chapter Seven

Neve needed to fortify her boundaries after movie night with her sisters, their significant others, Lottie, and Zelda's soon-to-be stepdaughter, Harper. She'd worried about the crowd being too large, but Isobel gave the okay since they were family and would wear masks for prevention.

The evening had been fun, to an extent. Gil had such an easy relationship with both Cash and Troy that Neve could envision future gatherings with her family that included the father of her baby. That part had heartened her, and focusing on those thoughts had kept her from casting too many lingering looks at Gil in the darkened family room of her cabin.

Yet there was a level of awkwardness. All of their guests had spent the whole evening looking at her and Gil with curious eyes until she started to question the wisdom of waiting to tell them about the baby.

One look at Lottie reminded Neve of the need to keep everyone focused on the child's surgery.

Now she intended to forge ahead and make the most of her rescheduled date with Gil to the Enchanted Forest holiday party at the local tree farm. She imagined he needed a distraction as well from his father's surgery scheduled two days from now. He hadn't spoken about it much, but she knew his bond with his father was strong. No doubt he worried.

More than a few eyes had tracked them on their way out of the Top Dog Dude Ranch, then again after they arrived at the tree farm. The business, owned by Ian Greer and his wife, Gwen, who also managed the ranch gift shop, was alight with holiday cheer. Rows of live firs, some still in the ground and others freshly cut, were illuminated by strands of lights. Poinsettias lined shelves in front of the small red barn office, along with piles of fresh greenery to frame mantels and doors. The scent of pine hung thick in the air, the fresh snowfall still clinging to needles, making the night all the more magical.

Alongside Gil, she walked deeper into the grove, waving to the Greer family from a distance. Then smiling at the school librarian and her crew next. Going out together tonight would start tongues wagging. Sure, they'd been spotted together in the sleigh on the caroling night. Their next outing in just a few days, however, would definitely give the impression they were a couple.

But it would also set the stage for when they finally made the baby announcement. Maybe then it wouldn't come as such a shock to those around them. They'd even sat together for supper in the ranch's dining hall before leaving. Her sisters were giving her some space for now, but she knew they would barrage her with questions soon enough.

Gil paused, pointing to the spot where Santa sat on a tractor for photos. "Do you want to take a picture and make your wish?"

A decorative mailbox waited to receive those letters for the North Pole, festive bows tied to the flag in the shape of a tree. While some might have a long wish list, her own needs were quite simple right now. A healthy baby. A safe pregnancy.

And some kind of harmony with Gil, now that they were linked for life. "I wouldn't want the children to have to wait longer while I took a turn."

Her gaze tracked over his handsome face, his brown eyes stirring the attraction that was never far from the surface.

"Fair point," he conceded as he skimmed a stray strand of her hair back into her hat.

A banjo player plucked out carols with a twang. Kids danced and twirled in the aisles, while adults searched for the perfect tree. The echo of their giggles and squeals, oohs and aahs, filled the air.

But what drew her attention most? A vintage pickup truck with a sign to collect toys for children in foster homes. While she held their two cups of warm apple cider, Gil carried a large cardboard box filled with donated presents to be wrapped and tagged. He solemnly set their offering in the truck bed.

Each package contained a removable tag listing the

contents. Remote-control dinosaur. Play-Doh kitchen. Blocks. LEGOs. On and on... He'd spent a fortune.

She knew he was adopted and he'd discussed it in passing, but right now, looking at that container full of presents for children who'd lost their families, her heart squeezed for them.

And for him. "How old were you when you were adopted?"

He nudged the box farther in to make room for future donations. "Five years old." He tipped his head toward her. "You look surprised."

"Not surprised, exactly." She struggled for the right words, ones that wouldn't make him feel awkward. "I'm just wondering how that detail never came up in conversation."

His hand lingered on the cargo bed of the pickup for a heartbeat. "I don't talk about those early years very often."

"I don't want to pry." But she wanted to know more.

In fact, she wondered why she'd never thought to ask before. She stepped over to a refreshments table, tucked between two life-size wooden soldiers, and ladled a refill of apple cider from a Crock-Pot. She dropped a cinnamon stick in each before passing him one.

"It's not prying. We're supposed to be using this time to get to know each other better." He took the drink then palmed the small of her back and steered her gently along a corridor of Fraser firs. "My biological mother gave me up for adoption. She was a young, single mom, working double overtime. Then she lost her job. The way I heard it, one problem after another hit, and she decided I needed a more financially stable life."

"That had to have been so difficult." She cradled her cup in both hands taking comfort from the warmth. "My heart breaks for you and for her."

His eyebrows pinched together as he stirred a cinnamon stick through his drink. "Please don't pity me. I don't have many memories of her. Just the scent of her shampoo, a faint echo of her voice singing me to sleep."

"Five years old is pretty young." Although she remembered vividly losing her favorite rabbit when she was that age and crying her eyes out for days. She couldn't imagine if she'd lost a parent.

He nodded slowly, his eyes seeming to look inward to old memories for a moment before he spoke. "The odd thing is that I didn't even remember those things until my adoptive mother passed away. Loss triggering loss, I guess."

Tears stung her eyes for him and the little boy he'd been, for the adult man who still carried around the ache. She stopped under an arbor of greenery, dotted with holly berries, and she gave him the space to think before he continued. Because clearly something more was knocking around inside his mind.

Music drifted along the wind, mixed with the happy voices and giggles of carefree shoppers. Here in their temporary haven, though, she realized Gil didn't give himself many quiet moments in life. Could he be outrunning these thoughts that caused him pain?

Certainly something she would have to mull over later. Right now, though, she focused on this man and his serious face cast in shadows.

"Neve, I need for you to know that I fully intend to be a part of this baby's life. No child of mine is growing up not knowing me."

She leaned into his touch, warm and stirring even through his gloves. She nodded and his arm dropped back to his side.

"Of course. I understand." She'd never really doubted him on that front. She just couldn't see a clear path on how they would handle such a complicated future. "We don't need to hammer out all the details right now. Remember, this is supposed to be a low-key time to celebrate Christmas, make it past the transplant surgery, and get to know each other better. We have months left to figure this out."

"Months? Not the way I see it." His cheeks puffed with a long exhale. "You're heading back to your job in a few short weeks. And my life is here."

Why was he pushing this now, especially after such a lovely evening together? Could he be sabotaging their relationship before they even had a couple of fragrant spruces loaded in the back of his pickup? "Are you asking me to change places of employment?"

"There are colleges here." He pointed out, then looked surprised at his own words.

She tamped down the urge to bristle and explained

logically, "It's not that simple. Even if there was an opening and I got hired, it's unlikely to match the pay and benefits I have now."

His palms slid from her slight shoulders and he linked hands with her. "And what about the *benefit* of our child living near both parents?"

"Well, we have whitewater rafting in North Carolina," she noted with a saucy smile in return. "You can be the one to move."

She dumped her cider and pivoted back toward the festivities, too aware of his gaze on her. Finally, she heard the crunch of his boots on gravel and he pulled up alongside her.

"I'm sorry," he said. "I broke the rules for our outing. Can we call a truce?"

She grasped his apology wholeheartedly. "Of course, even though I wouldn't qualify that as an argument."

"Thank you for being so gracious." He stroked along her jaw, his eyes holding hers for so long she thought he might kiss her again.

Ached for him to do so.

Then his hand slid away. "Let's check out the reindeer petting zoo, in honor of Rudy."

"Sounds like a perfect idea." She latched on to his suggestion eagerly, needing to put behind the weighty talk of things she couldn't yet reconcile.

But the image of that five-year-old boy losing his mama still stayed burned into her brain and on her heart.

* * *

After thirty years as an army nurse, Priscilla Kincaid needed peace. The job posting in Moonlight Ridge, Tennessee, had seemed too good to be true. A temporary stint, caring for a man who'd donated a kidney to a young girl. Apparently, finding short-term assistance over the holidays had proved challenging for him.

She put her SUV into Park in front of River Jack Hadley's mountain home. She'd come to his house for a pre-op interview, to make sure their expectations and his requirements were clearly stated up front. She grabbed her leather portfolio from the passenger seat and stepped from the vehicle, careful to avoid a patch of ice.

The place was larger than she'd expected. He had such a mountain man vibe to him, she'd thought he would live in more of a back-to-nature, minimalist home. He'd even called it a cabin, but it was more of a sprawling house, with pine planks rather than logs. Winding stairways wrapped around the three levels, with garland and lights along the railings. She made a note on her tablet of the significant slip hazard for someone recovering from a major operation.

She picked her way along the narrow path, grabbing hold of trees. Frozen pine cones crunched underfoot as she walked closer. The walkout basement sported a sign on the door that broadcast Gems by River Jack.

So he worked out of his basement? That would make keeping him off the stairs even more difficult.

One step at a time, Priscilla carefully climbed to the main floor. She hadn't hesitated to put in her application. She didn't need the money, since she had her military retirement. But the prospect of facing Christmas alone had her sinking into a depression she could ill afford after all the hard work she'd put in to overcome combat stress.

Meeting him at the bonfire had caught her by surprise. She just hadn't expected that man to be her age and enticing. Not a professional start to her new gig.

She climbed the last step and caught her breath at the workout. Not too long ago, she'd been able to keep pace in PT with new recruits.

Retirement was slowing her down, which gave her too much time for dark thoughts.

Stopping at the door, she pressed the bell and admired the wreath made of twisted wires with clear crystals. Unique. And surprising, like the home.

The front door swung open releasing a gust of warmth, and she relegated distracting thoughts to the far corners of her mind. "Good afternoon, Mr. Hadley."

"Jack, call me Jack, or River Jack. I'll answer to either one." He motioned her inside with the sweep of a hand, his fingers and palm bearing thin nicks and scars, no doubt from his jewel work. "Welcome to my home. Let me take your coat."

She eyed his thick, curly gray hair with surprise.

He'd been wearing a hat when they'd met before. He moved with an easy athleticism, his jeans and chambray shirt every bit as unassuming as his offhanded comment of living in a "cabin."

But his eyes? Those glittered like the gemstones he crafted into works of art.

"Thank you," she said, unwinding her scarf, then tugging off her gloves. She set her tablet on the entryway table before passing over her jacket. "I brought my tablet for us to review some paperwork, then I can email copies to you."

"Efficient. Would you like some coffee?"

"No, thank you. I had two cups at breakfast. Anything more than that makes me jittery." She took in the soaring ceiling and massive stone fireplace. Comfortable leather sofas, but with a high-end edge. Framed paintings of caverns filled the walls. Apparently, jewelry making paid very well. "Let's get right down to business. Give me a tour of the house and we can discuss the best way forward to get you back on your feet as soon as possible."

"Best way forward?" He rocked back on his heels, then followed her into the great room.

She turned as she strolled, making note of the wide, electric recliner. That could make for easier resting during the day, not having to use muscles to move it up and down. "Well, based on the floorplan of your home, we can decide where would be best for you to sleep."

"Uh, my own bed," he answered with a grumpy

laugh, leading her past an oak dining table to the kitchen.

The state-of-the-art space had appliances that appeared rarely used. She recalled from his forms that he ate most meals at the dude ranch with his son.

"Of course resting in your own room would be the ideal choice." This wasn't the first time she'd faced the issue with a patient. "As long as that doesn't require stairs. And how the shower is configured matters."

He smiled, a stubborn glint lighting his blue eyes. "I'll take your recommendations under consideration."

Hands on her hips, she resurrected her best army-soldier voice. "Mr. Hadley, I don't tell you how to make jewelry because you're the expert. And you should consider that this is my area of expertise. My job is to get you on your feet as soon as is safely possible."

"I'm healthy as a horse," he groused, leading her down a narrow hallway to a small study full of books and a daybed. "And I can guarantee you, I won't be sleeping in here."

Her mouth twitched. "Mr. Hadley, has anyone ever told you that you are not a compliant patient?"

"The night nurse my son wants me to hire said pretty much the same thing."

"Good for them." She nodded in approval. "I'm glad to know I won't be on this uphill battle alone."

"I guess I failed to mention that was only the first part of what she said. Right before she stated she wasn't interested in the job." He led her across the hall to the primary suite, a luxury space that more than met the requirements for recovery.

Her concerns about the stairs faded. She wished all her patients had these resources. "Who is the service sending to replace her?"

"Don't know." He adjusted a framed photo on the bedside table, a family-group shot from long ago, in matching holiday wear. "I don't need anyone while I'm asleep. I can always call Gil to come over."

She stole a quick peek into the bathroom and added another document tab on her device. "What times will he be here?"

"When I call him."

Typing in notes, she shook her head. "You're not making it easy to do my job."

"My work calms my spirit." He tapped a heavy blue crystal ring on his right hand that looked like something she'd once seen in a deployment to Turkey. "Surely, that's healing?"

She could sense he was the type who needed a little latitude in order to keep him from making larger mistakes. "If you do it sitting down, I can't see what harm there would be in that."

"Music to my ears." He rubbed his hands together and started toward the hall. "I'll make the first piece for you. What would you like? Earrings? A pendant? A charm to hang from your rearview mirror?"

She raced to keep up, past the office, down a different corridor to the great room. "You don't need to do that for me. You're already paying me."

"Well, I'm going to make something regardless, so you might as well place your order."

He was a nice guy.

The thought blindsided her and complicated her job.

Priscilla of the past would have asked him out on a date. But the old Priscilla had faded on the battlefield. The new version of herself managed to put one foot in front of the other by staying numb. "Perhaps a small good-luck charm for my keychain would be lovely. Thank you."

Something to ward off the nightmares. But that would be sharing too much.

"Consider your order placed." He rocked back on his boot heels again. "What's your favorite color?"

"Surprise me."

"You're making this a challenge."

"Then, maybe we're evenly matched." The words tumbled out too easily. She cleared her throat. "Professionally speaking."

"Of course. Maybe so."

From the return of that glint in his gorgeous blue eyes, she could tell he welcomed a challenge. And she absolutely did not need or welcome conflict in her life anymore.

She'd survived enough turmoil for two lifetimes.

Gil hadn't worn matching pj's since his mother planned a Christmas-card photo shoot. A memory he hadn't thought of in years, and one that he shuffled aside now for the grief and loss that went with it.

Better to focus on the here and now as he stood in the middle of a barn party with Neve, wearing matching reindeer pajamas, complete with a hoody sporting little antlers.

When he'd invited Neve to spend this evening with him, she already had plans to help her sister Zelda with the ranch's Holiday PJ Party. She didn't have time for lunch prior, since she needed to drive into town to pick out something to wear.

He'd offered to drive.

And now he was a human Rudolph in the middle of a cluster of people wearing coordinating plaid. Red-and-black was definitely the most popular pattern, whether in sleep pants or onesies. Some opted to stay in jeans while wearing the same sweatshirts, such as We Are Family with the year. Another had a tree pattern of cartoon faces, each labeled with a name.

The Purl Girls, not to be outdone, had knitted their own sweaters to wear with snowflake-patterned sleep pants. In perfect sync, they were leading line dances to a country version of "Feliz Naughty Dogs."

Troy Shaw ambled his way over, wearing a long sleeved T-shirt with a cow and Moo-ey Christmas in a thought bubble, just like his teenage daughter and fiancée. "Nice costume."

Gil flipped the hoodie back down to give his antlers a break. "I guess I didn't get the memo that T-shirts were allowed."

"I think you got suckered. But I suspect your ego can handle it."

Gil leaned against a rough-hewn support post. "What can I say? I wore what I was told."

The music shifted to "Jingle Paws," with Neve passing out bells to shake as they gathered for a puppet show on the far side from the dancing.

Troy shook his head, chuckling. "Next thing you know, they'll be singing 'Have a Holly Collie Christmas.'"

"Or 'Bark, the Herald Angels Sing.'"

Troy shot back. "'We Woof You a Merry Christmas.'"

"Good one." Gil applauded softly. "I missed this party last year. I was setting up the live nativity with a petting zoo."

Would he be bringing his child to either of the events in years to come? Or would he have to drive to North Carolina to spend the holiday with his daughter or son? Certainly his suggestion that Neve move here permanently had gone over like a load of bricks.

He understood her point. But he still had a whole host of reasons why they'd be better off in Moonlight Ridge. He'd tucked away those talking points for another day.

As the song and chimes faded, Zelda's voice drifted over as she kept the kids entertained during the puppet show prep. "Why did the dog get coal in his/her stocking?" She paused, then declared, "He/she had a ruff year."

The kids burst into giggles, rolling on the floor in a tangle of red-and-green sleepwear.

Neve leaned forward conspiratorially, the basket of reclaimed bells in her hands. "What did the dog say when he lost the bone he got in his stocking?" She waited for a beat, then winked. "It's been nice gnawing you."

A little boy with a buzzed haircut jumped to his feet and shouted, "Know why Frosty turned yellow?" He barely paused to catch his breath. "The little dog over there lifting a leg beside him can tell you."

The kids responded with a mix of *ewwws* and laughs.

Troy smothered a smile. "That's my kind of kid."

Gil couldn't argue with that. He scrubbed a hand over his jaw. "I wish Lottie could have come. She would have loved this."

Troy's grin faded. "Before long, she'll be healthier than ever and I intend to help her make up for lost time. I have my eye on a pony for her from Aunt Zelda and Uncle Troy." He clapped Gil on the shoulder. "Looks like the puppet show is ready to start and so I'm on proud-dad duty. Harper is the narrator. Catch you later?"

"You bet." He stepped back, scanning for Neve.

He spotted her tucking the basket under a table loaded with assorted holiday treats, like caramel popcorn, mint brownies, and gingerbread men. She stood and grabbed a napkin, surveying the spread.

Maybe he'd been approaching this all wrong in

being so serious with the get-to-know-you questions and diving into the past. Perhaps he needed to revert to the more lighthearted tone when they'd first met. When they'd forged an indelible connection.

Weaving past an inflatable Santa, he stopped just behind her and whispered, "Hey gorgeous. Wanna play Spin the Candy Cane?"

She glanced over her shoulder and rolled her eyes. "Please don't tell me that line has worked for you in the past."

"I've never tried it before." He reached past her to snag a piece of peppermint bark.

"I think I'm complimented. Maybe." Her eyebrows pinched together and she shook her head. "No, on second thought, I've decided it's an insult to my intelligence."

The words carried a teasing air he'd missed. He took heart and pressed on. "You're smoking hot when you're in professor mode."

Her shoulders braced and she pressed a finger to her lips, tracing slowly. Enticingly. "I'm always in professor mode. That's who I am."

"That's why you're already hot." He grinned, and when she didn't put him in his place, he continued, "And I can think of a time or two when you were far from buttoned-up."

The simmering awareness flowed between them, as powerful as ever. Which should have been ironic, given they were both wearing a reindeer onesie. What would she think when she opened the surprise gift he'd left on her kitchen counter just before they'd left for the party? After they'd bought their pj's, he'd gone back and bought a matching set for Rudy.

And as fast as the flash from the nearby photo booth, the warmth faded as the memory of a long-ago matching picture taken with his dad and mom returned full force.

It had hung in the living room for years afterward, until his dad had quietly removed it, perhaps in deference to his own grief.

The mental image of that photo remained, however. Seeing it in his mind's eye now. An image that made his gut twist with all he'd lost. All he could still lose when his father went under the knife.

And how much more of his heart he risked once he and Neve shared a child.

Chapter Eight

Neve decided the best way to take her mind off her own worries would be to focus on her sister. Which explained how she ended up blending yogurt, honey, and cucumber for a homemade face mask.

She'd planned the sister afternoon at her cabin, an opportunity to pamper Isobel while Lottie napped under Cash's watchful care. The afternoon served a dual purpose of treating themselves while also making gifts for the hospital staff. Isobel never missed an opportunity to recognize the caregivers entrusted with her daughter.

With a final tap of the blender, Neve called over to her sisters, "Could one of you pass me those three little bowls by the coffee maker?"

"Got it." Zelda popped to her feet from the kitchen table, littered with craft supplies, dried flowers, and ribbons. They'd spent the afternoon making eucalyptus bath salts and peppermint lip balm, filling jars, and tying festive ribbons. The dining table sported a pyramid of their gifts. Hollie and Jacob had donated the supplies from the ranch's greenhouse and craft stash. They'd even added three Top Dog Dude Ranch robes for the sisters, a thoughtful gift during a stressful time.

As much as Neve had enjoyed the outings and ranch revelry, she appreciated quiet moments of Christmas prep, like this. A fire crackled in the hearth and her new tree filled a corner. She and Gil had each chosen one, although she hadn't yet found time to decorate beyond wrapping a string of twinkling lights. Although at night, those minimalist glimmers were magical.

Jazzy holiday tunes played softly while Rudy snoozed on his new dog bed. The puppy looked exceptionally adorable in his spiffy reindeer shirt. The present from Gil had caught her by surprise. There hadn't been a note. But she hadn't needed one to guess the giver. The dog shirt was a perfect match to the pj's they'd worn to the party.

Neve lined up the bowls on a tray before pouring the goopy mixture of homemade face mask into one dish after the other. "Fingers crossed this isn't a total disaster."

Isobel tied a sparkly ribbon around a bag of bath salts. "Gran would have said that sometimes the best fun could be found in the unscripted moments and detours."

"Amen," Zelda cheered, placing a plate of blueberry scones on the table and mugs of chai tea in front of her sisters before taking her seat.

Neve set her tray nearby, then nudged two small

bowls of the homemade goop to her sisters and pulled the third toward herself. Moving aside a basket of dried sage, she revealed a bag of headbands to protect their hair.

Matching, of course.

A quick selfie later, Neve tugged on plastic gloves, then scooped a small amount in the palm of her hand and began to smooth the cool ingredients along her cheeks. "I would have suggested the ranch's spa, but I've used up all my vouchers for the month. And honestly, I prefer to have the sister time away from everyone else."

Isobel smeared the creamy mixture along her forehead. "You're sweet to do this for me."

Zelda sniffed the bowl and smiled blissfully. "We thought you needed some pampering." She dabbed the mixture under her eyes. "You've been doing so much with work and for Lottie. For a few hours, let us look after you."

Isobel's jaw trembled for a moment before she drew in a steadying breath and went back to covering her face. "I would argue about doing my fair share, but I'm so thankful to have the distraction from thinking about the surgery."

How was Gil handling the stress of worrying about his father? A twinge of guilt pinched. She'd been so focused on the baby—and her niece—that she hadn't given near enough concern to the weight he must be carrying as well. She wished she could do something for Gil, like take Rudy over for a visit in his new shirt, except he was going straight from work to spend time with his father this evening.

Her gaze skated to the refrigerator with a photo anchored by a paw-print clip, the picture taken at the Holiday PJ Party of the two of them dancing with their reindeer hoods up. He'd been such a good sport when she'd chosen the most embarrassing outfit possible.

She peeled off her gloves and picked up her phone, snapping a quick picture of Rudy and texting it to Gil.

Isobel reached for her chai tea, her face now fully slathered with the white face mask. "This is all perfect. It's been a stressful few weeks…months really, with the waiting. And trying not to imagine the worst-case scenario…"

Zelda patted Isobel's hand, compassion creasing her forehead. "Let's not defeat the purpose of our relaxing afternoon by talking about the future. Let's make the most of our time together before Neve leaves us after the New Year."

Had her sister meant to guilt her into staying? Neve decided to ignore the pressure. "Pass the scones, please. And the cream."

Zelda nudged the whole tray closer. "I bet they don't make scones like this in North Carolina."

Lifting an eyebrow in subtle warning, only to feel a little of her yogurt mask slide too close to her eye, Neve patted her napkin near the spot before spooning lemon cream on a scone. "Do they do fireworks for New Year's here? I think I remember them from the Fourth of July. Or is it considered a fire hazard?"

Isobel spooned jam onto her pastry. "I seem to recall Cash telling me that they are and he'll be working that evening. But they'll shoot them off over the lake—for safety—like on Independence Day."

Zelda broke a scone in half. "And there's a big party in one of the barns, along with a bonfire outside. I hear that New Year's traditions are quite the rage around here."

Thinking of that flip of the calendar made nerves twitter inside her. As much as she loved her job, leaving became more complicated by the day. "Like a balloon drop at midnight?"

Isobel dabbed a crumb from the corner of her mouth. "Hollie had me help with the write-up for the local newspaper. They'll be serving a meal of black-eyed peas and rice for luck. Making noise at midnight is supposed to scare away bad spirits."

Neve frowned, toying with the tie on her fluffy robe, too aware that she wouldn't be able to hide her pregnancy much longer. "I didn't realize that was the purpose of the horns and such."

Nodding, Isobel continued, "Apparently, the locals embrace old traditions and the ranch plays into that regional lore. Everyone gets a special Top Dog Dude Ranch coin to place in the sink. When you wash your face there, it's supposed to bring wealth."

"Ah," Zelda said. "I'll have to fish out three quarters to put in the sink when we clear off these masks."

Isobel smiled, creasing the drying paste on her face. "Hollie had a slew more traditions listed, like throwing out an old calendar. Those who wish for travel will run seven laps around their cabin. And my favorite..." She leveled a gaze at Neve. "Eat twelve grapes while sitting under a table and you'll find love."

Neve winced. They were definitely ganging up on her today, and since she'd hosted at her cabin, she couldn't leave early. "I'm a woman of science, not superstition."

Zelda gulped down a bite before saying, "But you also have Gran's DNA. That comes with at least a touch of belief in the mystical."

Neve bit her tongue to keep from ruining the afternoon. It wasn't her sisters' fault she was on edge from things she'd chosen not to tell them.

Zelda's brow furrowed with contrition. "I'm sorry. I didn't mean to push a sore subject. I just thought that you and Gil... Never mind. I'm going to stop before I put my foot in it even worse."

Isobel clapped her hands together, dusting off scone crumbs. "Time to gather those coins and wash off this goop, because if someone walked in, they might mistake us for a Moonlight Ridge woodland creature."

Neve appreciated the way her sisters could shift the mood rather than sinking into contemplation like she did. Having a more lighthearted approach could sometimes work as well as a long walk in the woods to reduce stress. And they all needed a diversion from thinking about the morning's surgery.

She reached for her phone. "Forget about hiding. Before we wash our faces, we need a selfie."

* * *

As the morning dragged on waiting for news, Gil drank his third cup of crummy coffee. The doctors had indicated surgery would take four to six hours.

They were currently at five. His father's surgery to remove the kidney had gone well, and now they waited for news about Lottie's procedure.

Hospitals decorated for the holidays always seemed strange to him. The antiseptic scent and lack of color had been splashed with fake tinsel stretched along the wall, up and down, like a heart-monitor line. For some reason, the artificial tree in any medical building always looked about three seasons past its prime.

This little sad Charlie Brown tree was no exception.

Neve sat in the industrial chair beside him, her laptop open as she typed away on final edits to her textbook. Zelda and Troy shared earbuds as they watched something on their phone.

Isobel was curled up against Cash with her head on his shoulder. Her eyes were shut as if she couldn't bear to process even the scene around her. Cash kept his arm around her shoulder, rubbing her slowly while he studied the newscast. His tight jaw relayed a world of tension.

A few other folks had come and gone from the waiting area this morning, but at the moment it was just the six of them. He could hear the nurses speaking in low voices at the station nearby, their activity a well-coordinated dance as they moved in and out of their small base.

Checking the clock on the wall, again, Gil swallowed down bile. He'd always been healthy. He'd only come to the hospital to have his arm set after a skiing mishap, to visit a friend having an appendectomy...

And when his mother had died.

The accident had been so sudden he and River Jack hadn't even made it to the emergency room before she passed away.

He downed the rest of his java, crushed the cup in a frustrated fist, and focused on the present. His father would be fine. Lottie would thrive.

This day would not end in tragedy.

Leaning to the side, he pitched his cup into the garbage can. He straightened just as Neve closed her laptop and set it aside to clasp his hand.

"Could I get you some more coffee?" she asked, squeezing his fingers.

"I should probably lay off it. Thanks though." He stroked his thumb across her wrist.

"Of course. Your father is in there," she said, her forehead furrowing with concern. "This has to be impossibly difficult for you."

"And your niece. Today is, well, a lot."

Her throat moved in an emotional swallow. "Nobody ever imagines themselves in this situation."

Sliding doors swished open, and he bolted upright, as did Lottie's folks. Only to find it wasn't a doctor, but rather the nurse his father had hired.

Priscilla Kincaid strode closer, sneakers squeaking along the tile floor. "Gil, have you heard anything yet about River Jack?"

"Nothing so far," Gil said, weary with worry.

Neve nodded toward Priscilla's surgical scrubs. "I didn't know you worked here too?"

"Technically, I don't. I was sitting with a client on the third floor and just finished up." Sitting beside him, she fidgeted with her lanyard, her silver-blond hair in a tight braid looking none the worse for wear after her long shift. "I thought I would come down and check how your father's doing. And Lottie, too, of course."

Gil nodded. "That's thoughtful of you. I'll be sure to let Dad know."

Neve reached into her canvas sack and pulled out a little gift bag. "My sisters and I made these to show our appreciation to the people caring for Lottie—and River Jack, too, of course. Some bath salts and lip balm."

Priscilla's brown eyes widened in pleased surprise. "Thank you so much. You didn't have to do that, but I'm certainly appreciative." She tucked the gift away in her backpack. "Some days I vow my skin still hasn't recovered from so much time out in the desert."

Neve set her canvas sack beside her laptop. "The desert? You lived out west?"

"I was stationed in the Middle East," Priscilla answered. "I was an army nurse, before I received a medical discharge."

Gil latched on to the conversational shift, welcoming a diversion. "My dad served as well. In the Army Reserve."

"I didn't know that." She smoothed a hand along her hair. "It will give us something to talk about while he's recovering. How long has he been in surgery?"

"A little over five hours," he said, nerves taking a fresh bite out of his stomach.

Her gaze darted to the door where doctors should be walking through...

At her nervous gesture, Gil wondered if Priscilla Kincaid had more than a professional interest in his dad. The random thought knocked him for a loop, as his father hadn't dated since becoming a widower. Or at least, not that Gil knew about. If so, maybe his father had been keeping the information secret to keep from upsetting him.

Not that Gil had an objection, he just hadn't considered the possibility. Had he taken his dad for granted? The notion brought a swell of guilt for not considering his father's loneliness, with decades left to live.

Man, he was a mess and needed to get his head together for his dad and for Neve. But in this moment, he feared he'd fallen far short of River Jack's example.

The sound of swishing doors jerked him back to reality just as a pair of doctors walked through the door.

River Jack pushed through the fog and blinked his eyes open, confused for a moment. The crisp sheets felt alien, the ceiling not at all like his mountain home.

The walls were too stark, the sheets too itchy. And the *beep, beep, beep* wasn't an alarm exactly...

Hospital.

He was in a hospital.

For a moment he panicked, imagining he was back in the emergency room that fateful day when his wife had been broadsided at a stop sign. She'd died at the scene, but they'd resuscitated her, only to have her crash again in the emergency room. He'd never had the chance to say goodbye.

The fog parted a bit, if not the grief, and he remembered.

Surgery. Except this time he wasn't here because a life had been lost. But because he'd saved one.

At least, he hoped so.

Realization slithered the rest of the way through the anesthesia haze. The steady chirp of the not-alarm-clock, heart monitor, almost soothed him back to sleep. But something tugged harder at him to stay awake. He needed to find out about Lottie's surgery.

Another part of him was afraid to hear, in case it hadn't gone well. What if somehow he'd been too late to help her?

Adjusting the oxygen tubes hooked around his ears, he looked around the room, searching for a call button and saw his son. Gil slept in the industrial recliner, so River Jack gave himself a moment more to get his bearings while his son napped.

A homemade card from Lottie rested on his rolling tray. She'd colored a picture of the two of them, side by side with Cocoa. Lottie had written a big red "thank you" across the front and signed the inside. Stickers covered the inside and outside, jewelry and puffy gemstones.

The weight of the honor he'd been given, being able to help this little girl, overwhelmed him. Not just because he'd been a match for her. But also because the community of Moonlight Ridge had brought all of them together in a convoluted family tree that had somehow managed to thrive. Maybe it was the mystical power of that spring on the Top Dog Dude Ranch. Or perhaps it was the strength of the caring, good people who populated the place.

All he knew? He'd felt blessed to be a part of Lottie's journey.

And while he'd been willing to make whatever sacrifice necessary for that little girl, he was thankful to be alive. He couldn't bear for his son to suffer another loss. Gil presented himself as fearless, reckless even, but there'd been a vulnerability in him from the moment River Jack had knelt in front of him and introduced himself.

Time to find out about Lottie.

River Jack tried to talk, but his mouth was dry, his throat sore from intubation. He cleared his throat and tried again.

"Son?" he said, voice croaky and soft. "Lottie? How's she doing?"

Gil sat up sharply, blinking fast, then leaning to

clasp his father's hand. "She's doing great, Dad. Everything went best-case scenario for her and for you."

River Jack exhaled hard, relief surging through him. "Then, the pain is more than worth it."

"Should I get the nurse?" He searched for the call button.

"No need. I'm fine for now," River Jack said, trying to move as little as possible. "Plenty drugged up."

Worry creased Gil's face. "What's your pain level? There's a chart on the wall over there."

"The pain will pass," he said, although right now he was starting to see the wisdom of that bossy nurse's words about limiting stairs. If his current discomfort was any indication, the recovery was going to be tougher than he'd anticipated.

Gil relented, sinking back into his chair. "Well, let me know if anything changes. I've been cleared to sit with you all night."

River Jack pointed to a basket by the sink, the tape on his IV tugging enough to pinch. "What's that stuff over there? With the big red bow on top?"

"Oh that?" He shot to his feet, all nervous energy, like when he'd been a kid, and brought the wicker container over. Gil sifted through the contents, all decked out with glittery ribbon. "Neve and her sisters made gifts for the hospital staff whenever they come by your room."

"Well, that was mighty thoughtful." He studied his son, wondering not for the first time how deep his feelings for Neve Dalton went. For sure, Gil had done a poor job at hiding his interest. River Jack just hoped his boy wasn't leading her on. "They're sweet girls, all three of them."

Gil dropped the little containers and bags back into the basket. "Your nurse stopped by to check on you. Priscilla Kincaid."

"She must have been working." He was nothing more than a patient to her, after all, a patient who hadn't listened to her concerns.

"That's what I thought at first." He set the container of gifts on the ugly orange sofa under the window. "She came to the waiting room after her shift with another client—just to ask about you. I'm relieved to have her help looking out for you while I'm at work."

Well, that had been kind of her. But still. He didn't enjoy thinking of himself as an invalid in need of a nurse. Especially one who'd intrigued him so thoroughly—before he found out she'd been assigned to care for him.

Of all the indignities.

In spite of the pain, he couldn't stop himself from insisting, "I can take care of myself, you know." He would just avoid the stairs. "All the literature says I'll be sleeping a lot while I recover."

How would he get any rest knowing Priscilla Kincaid was in his house, waiting to help him clamber his way to the bathroom?

Gil sighed, leaning forward, elbows resting on his knees. "Dad, do this for me." He drew in a ragged breath, shadows under his eyes as if he'd spent more than one sleepless night lately. "And for Mom. If she were the one in that bed and you couldn't care for her, you would insist on hiring a nurse."

River Jack flinched and wanted to chastise his son for the low blow in bringing up his mother. With the memories of that awful day two years ago still so fresh in his mind, the words stung all the more.

But also, with that loss hovering like a dark cloud in this sterile room, he reminded himself his son had suffered plenty too. The void in their lives could never be filled.

So he couldn't deny his son this request for additional caregiving. If River Jack died, Gil would have no one. "Okay then, son. Guess I'm at the healing mercy of the drill-sergeant nurse."

Chapter Nine

Neve had never felt so relieved and exhausted in her life.

The hospital vending machine in front of her thudded as it dispensed a can of fruit juice. She popped the top and gulped down the citrusy drink. The cold sugary flavor gave her a much-needed boost at the end of such a long and emotional day.

Her stomach grumbled and she needed a shower. A bed and nice, long night's sleep would be welcome too. But she needed to be sure Isobel had everything she needed for the night. Cash too.

And of course, Gil. This vending machine better be well stocked.

The hospital had quieted as most visitors left, the cafeteria and gift shop closing for the night. A nurse pushed a vitals machine, the rattles echoing down the corridor. Her badge sported a sprig of holly. The corner television softly broadcast a home improvement show, the host sledge-hammering down a wall.

Thank heaven Lottie was responding better than expected to the new kidney. And when she'd woken from surgery, the little girl's first words had been concern for Mr. River Jack.

Neve's heart squeezed, and she slipped her credit card into the vending machine, glancing over at her sister. "What can I get for you? And don't say nothing. I won't rest easy until I know you're well stocked with food for the evening. Cash too."

Isobel chewed her bottom lip, hugging her sweater tighter around herself. "You choose. I don't have the mental bandwidth to make a decision."

It was the first time Isobel had left Lottie's side, but Cash had encouraged her to stretch her legs while Lottie slept. The vending machines were only a few feet away from her room, anyway.

"Can do," Neve said, selecting granola bars, dried fruit, and beef jerky. Three of everything—to include Gil. She knew he had to be wiped out, even if he didn't say the words. She'd been popping back and forth between Lottie and River Jack, and of course, checking on Gil. There hadn't been much time for talk since the doctors brought the good news.

But there had been plenty of hugs and tears of relief. Although once the adrenaline rush of joy settled, the exhaustion began to set in.

Isobel bent to retrieve the snacks from the vending machine. She tucked Cash's into her canvas bag stamped with a Cocoa's Caring Canine blog logo while keeping out a granola bar for herself. "Thank you for staying with me today. I don't know what I would have done without my sisters and Cash."

"I can stay as long as you need me to." Neve sealed her lips together, tight, to keep from yawning. Especially when her sister must be bone weary, and Neve was minutes away from heading home. Zelda and Troy were even giving her a ride.

"Thank you, but please go home and rest." She tore into the granola bar, chewing and swallowing fast. "You look exhausted. I'll need your help more when she's discharged, about a week from now, I hope."

"Well, tell my niece that I'm ready to spoil her rotten and watch all the princess movies she wants."

"I will. Thank you." Isobel walked backward and pointed over Neve's shoulder. "Your guy just came out and I think he wants to talk to you before you leave."

Neve didn't bother arguing with the characterization of Gil as her boyfriend. And even if she'd tried, Isobel had already started down the corridor, only pausing for a quick word with Gil before she took off again toward Lottie's room. Neve waited until her sister's footsteps faded before turning her attention to Gil.

Empathy for what he'd gone through—the stress and worry for his dad—struck her anew. River Jack might have been the one to donate a kidney, but his family had put their hearts on the line as well. Gil looked even more exhausted than she felt, and with good reason. He'd lost so many people in his life. This day must have tapped into those losses in such a painful way.

Forking his fingers through his tousled hair, he

closed the gap with long-legged strides. He stopped a simple hand's reach away, the little vending corner quiet and oddly intimate. "I heard you were still here. You should go home and get some rest. You need to take care of yourself."

She knew that she bristled because she was so tired. She bit back the urge to snap defensively. "I could say the same to you." She passed his energy bar and drink over. "I just wanted to give you these snacks before I leave."

"That's really thoughtful." Gil tucked the granola bar into his shirt pocket and unscrewed the water bottle. "Thanks. I missed getting down to the cafeteria before it closed, so this is a lifesaver."

Linking fingers with her, he drew her closer. "No offense, but you look exhausted."

Neve stifled a yawn, leaning into him ever so slightly. "You wouldn't be wrong. How about you?"

"I'm going to stay here for the night." His thumb circled along the inside of her wrist, gently, enticingly. "I was worried about the icy roads at night. You can use my truck."

"I'm actually catching a ride with Troy and Zelda. She'll give me a ride back in the morning to see Lottie and retrieve my car. Thanks for checking though." His touch and thoughtfulness stirred butterflies inside her until she remembered the gravity of the day. "How's your father?"

"Weaker than I expected, which is scary." A ragged sigh wracked through him. "My dad's usually so…"

"Full of life?" Like his son. She cradled Gil's face in her hand, his jaw bristly against her skin.

He angled toward her and kissed her palm, before pulling her to his side. "He doesn't regret a thing though. He's already trying to talk his way out of having a nurse."

A delicious shiver rippled through her at his romantic gesture. "I hope you persuaded him otherwise."

"Absolutely." He rested his forehead against hers. "I know you were here for your niece and your sister, but it really meant a lot to me having you here."

"I wouldn't have been anywhere else." She arched up onto her toes to kiss him, lingering only for a moment. It was more of a comfort connection, than the ones of passion they'd shared in the past. But there was still an intimacy, of connection, to the moment that wasn't lost on her.

She wanted to blame her feelings on the emotional day, except she was finding it tougher and tougher to step out of Gil's arms.

Gil had spent far too much time sitting around over the past three days, so he welcomed the activity of prepping his dad's house for his homecoming tomorrow morning. Thank heaven.

Breathing a sigh of relief, he smoothed the freshly washed quilt over his dad's bed. He glanced at his watch and jogged down the steps to the basket of bath towels on the sofa. Maybe it had been overkill to re-wash the linens, but he worried about his father getting an infection.

Three folded towels later, the doorbell rang, the chimes echoing "Deck the Halls." Frowning, he strode to the door and spotted a figure illuminated by the sidelights... Neve. His mind flooded with the memories of their simple but moving kiss by the vending machine. Not the most romantic of locales, but the moment left its mark all the more for the impulsiveness, for the ease with which they fit together. For the comfort she had sought in him, with him.

He tugged the heavy front door open and drank in the sight of her, balm for his exhausted spirit. From her shiny dark hair to her beautiful smile, lighting her blue eyes. Her slight but shapely body, with curves accentuated by pregnancy.

Without hesitation or second thoughts, he drew her into his arms and breathed in the minty scent of her shampoo. He nuzzled her ear, then brushed his mouth over hers. Her hum of pleasure encouraged him to deepen the kiss.

A thud startled him. Easing back, he saw her bag had hit the ground. He leaned to scoop it up—a heavy, insulated bag. "What do you have there?"

"Oh, uh," she said, shrugging out of her red wool coat, "I brought a couple of casseroles and baked goods for your dad. And for you too. I had blueberry scones the other day—from the ranch bakery—and they were amazing. I thought your dad might like some too."

"If he doesn't eat them, I sure will." Carrying the box for her, he motioned her through toward the kitchen, enjoying the gentle sway of her hips in her long sweater dress.

She glanced over her shoulder at him, her ponytail swishing. "This place is stunning. I didn't realize how large it would be. Your dad always refers to his home as a cabin, so I envisioned something more along the lines of the Top Dog Dude Ranch guest houses."

"My dad is an unpretentious man." He set the insulated bag on the counter beside a Santa Gnome cookie jar. "It's one of the things I admire most about him. As for the size of the house, he made some wise investments and also saved by putting in sweat equity. Most of the building materials he used were locally sourced."

He skimmed his palm over the pale oak cutting board island, remembering how his father refinished it to just the shade his mom requested.

"Gran would have been proud to hear that." She unzipped the sack and pulled out the contents one by one, passing him two casseroles for the freezer. "I wish they could have met—and that you could have known her too."

He tucked the casseroles on a shelf, noting the otherwise-sparse pickings for the first time. The lasagna and chicken Alfredo would come in handy, but he made a mental note to go shopping all the same.

Shaking off the distraction, he focused on his time

with Neve. "Thank goodness your grandmother made sure you and your sisters came here."

"For the longest time, my sisters and I thought she'd made up most of the tales of Moonlight Ridge. She would show us her crystal ring and tell us about the gems in Sulis Cave. We thought she was just embellishing childhood memories." She set the box of scones on the counter with a container of jam, her shoulder brushing his enticingly. "But to you those tales would have been normal stories since you're from here."

"I cut my teeth on the Legend of Sulis." The tale of how the founders of Moonlight Ridge who followed a doe into a cave, except the deer was actually the Queen of the Forest. They found a lost pup who was restored by the healing waters in the springs. "My dad took me to the cave often, to share about the different crystals inside."

Plucking one of the scones out for herself, she leaned back against the counter, nibbling. "Did you grow up in this house?"

She broke off a piece of the pastry and offered it to him, lifting it directly to his mouth to feed him herself. Her gaze held his intently.

His brain fogged at the brush of her finger across his lips. He swallowed the bit of scone without taking his eyes from hers. "Not this incarnation of it. The walkout basement is the only original part—a one-story house with two bedrooms. Dad drew up blueprints for the expansion, had them framed and hung on the wall."

"How lovely to have the tangible reminder of their dreams."

The brain haze faded as he recalled his parents so happy together then, not knowing the heartbreak waiting down the road. "He promised Mom that he would have the place finished before their retirement. Extra space to entertain the grandkids, he used to say."

It hadn't occurred to him until that moment that one of those grandchildren would be here very soon. He suspected River Jack would be thrilled. More so, however, if the mother of Gil's child was in the picture too.

"When did he complete the final addition?" She flattened a palm against his chest.

In comfort? He rested his hand over hers, anchoring the sensation. "Eighteen months before Mom died. He says he knows it's too big for him now, but he can't bring himself to sell it."

Her fingers pressed deeper, firmer. "I imagine that would be like a final goodbye of sorts."

"That's what he says."

Neve stepped closer, her forehead furrowed. "Do you mind if I ask how she died?" She patted his chest. "If it's too painful, please don't feel like you have to answer."

Flipping his hand, he linked their fingers, his heartbeat thudding against their clasped hands. "Car accident. A truck ran a stop sign and broadsided her vehicle. She didn't have a heartbeat when EMS arrived. They brought her back, but she still died in the emergency room. There wasn't time to process the seismic shift in our world. There still hasn't been enough time."

Her deep blue eyes filled with empathy. "That had to have made coming to the hospital for your father and Lottie's surgery even more unbearable."

"It wasn't a walk in the park, that's for sure," Gil said, cheeks puffing on an exhale, before he brushed aside the dark cloud threatening his time with Neve. "So Dad and Lottie will both be released tomorrow, and your ultrasound is in a couple of weeks. When do we tell our families?"

Maybe it had been the thought of River Jack's grandchild toddling down the halls of this echoing home that had made Gil all the more ready to share the news.

She blinked fast, then shrugged. "After the appointment with the doctor? If you want to tell them at the same time, we could do a video call instead, if your father isn't up to coming over to Lottie's."

"I realize that originally I wanted to let them know at the same time, but I didn't think about how we would have to be in two different places to do that. I would prefer that we tell them together." He hurried to add, "We can speak with your crew first, then come over to Dad's. I want our families to know that even if we're not a regular couple, we're still unified for our child."

Although right now, standing so close, they felt mighty like a couple. The memory of the nights they'd spent together filled the air.

She worried her bottom lip between her teeth before saying, "As long as we're clear with them. I don't need a bunch of matchmakers reading into our every move."

That would be a surefire way to blow up the fragile peace they'd found. Gil knew River Jack would be every bit as apt to matchmake as Neve's siblings. Not helpful, at all. "I agree with you on that."

She tipped her head to the side. "And about the kiss earlier…"

"Yes?" Wincing, he waited for the reminder they needed to keep their distance and objectivity. That they had a million-and-one reasons not to resume their affair. For the baby's sake. They needed to keep calm and balanced for the long term to co-parent their child.

A lump formed in his throat, the emotion so intense he almost missed the light glinting in her blue eyes. A light of excitement.

Twisting her fingers in his shirt, she tugged him closer. "I wouldn't mind one more kiss for the road."

Priscilla had always heard that dreams didn't have smells. But she hadn't found that to be true with her nightmares. The doctor said PTSD night terrors were different, in that rather than being a memory, it was as if the event was truly playing out for the first time.

Understanding didn't make her feel one bit better

as she woke with the scent of smoke and explosives in her nostrils.

Because where was the logic in dreams?

Forcing herself awake, she struggled to ground herself with her five senses.

Seeing River Jack's living room.

Feeling the cool leather of the sofa.

Tasting her lemon water in her YETI.

Hearing the crackle of the fire in the fireplace.

Smelling the evergreen scent of the Christmas tree.

So much for her first day on the job caring for her new patient. To be fair, she'd worked a twelve-hour shift since his son had to work late to make up for the time he'd missed for his father's surgery. She must have drifted off once River Jack started his nap.

Thank goodness he was still breathing deeply in his recliner, eyes closed. She took another drag on her lemon water, careful not to let the ice rattle, and set the thermos back on the end table. Then froze, the sense of being watched creeping over her. Just a symptom of her nightmare?

She scanned the room and found River Jack studying her.

"Hey," he asked, his voice still hoarse from the intubation, "are you okay? That was some doozy of a bad dream you were having."

"I'm so sorry." A lock of hair from her French braid slid free, and she tucked it behind her ear. "I'm embarrassed that I must have dozed off on the sofa. Looks like we both slept the day away."

A wall of windows showcased the distant valley as the last purple rays surrendered to night, stars just starting to flicker through. She walked to the towering Fraser fir in the corner and turned on the lights. His son had brought it by and strung the lights, apologizing for not bringing ornaments too. Holidays were busy enough, even without a major surgery.

The hum of the recliner whined as he adjusted from full recline to halfway sitting up. "You have nothing to apologize for. You pulled a long shift when my son had to stay late at work."

"I appreciate your being so forgiving." She shook her head. "But what if you had needed me?"

"Then, I would have called out, and you would have woken up. There's no reason for you to stare at me while I nap." His cheeks dimpled with a roguish grin. "That would be a little creepy."

A smile played at her mouth. "Well, isn't that what you were just doing? Watching me sleep?"

"Busted," he admitted.

A light smile at his humor dusted away a touch of the horror from her nightmare, if not all. "Well, you're not paying me to snooze."

"I'm paying for you to be available in a crisis and you're here." He tapped the armrest. "For example, where did my remote control wander off to? That's the kind of thing that would have me out of my chair and sprawled on the floor if you weren't around."

"That's kind of you." She fished his clicker off the floor by the recliner, then adjusted the blanket over his legs and grasped his wrist to take his pulse, needing the work to keep her thoughts from wandering into tricky territory.

She felt drawn to him, and it would be foolish to try to deny it.

"Sounded like quite the nightmare," he observed after a moment, his gaze fixed on her face.

Her heartbeat slugged harder.

"Hmm. Hold on. I'm counting." She used the excuse for time to gather her thoughts, because truth be told, she could check his heart rate with a brass band playing. Or a war zone. She knew that for a fact. "I get them sometimes, since I was in the service."

"Do you mean PTSD?" he said matter-of-factly.

And she appreciated that he didn't overdo the sympathy that would only make her feel self-conscious.

"Something like that." She released his wrist and busied herself with adjusting the throw pillows and straightening magazines.

"If you need to go home now, Gil should be here soon," he assured her. "He said something about putting a casserole in the microwave."

"I'm fine staying until he arrives. The roads are so unreliable this time of year, he may be delayed. But thank you for offering." She fidgeted, searching for something else to occupy herself. "I'll pop that casserole in the microwave so it's ready when he gets here." She made fast tracks to the kitchen, finding chicken Alfredo thawing in the neatly organized refrigerator.

She filled the silence by calling out, "Your son mentioned you had time in the service."

She asked to make conversation. Not because he fascinated her.

"Uh-huh." His raspy voice drifted from the other room. "The Reserves—Army."

"Right." She poured him a glass of spring water and made her way back into the toasty-warm living room. "What did you do in the military?"

"I was a geologist," he said simply. "I went overseas a few times, analyzing soil samples and offering recommendations for cleanup before rebuilding."

"That's fascinating." She reclaimed her seat on the sofa, tucking her legs to the side.

When she had initially reviewed his paperwork in her system, she'd had an idea that he was a creative type. Which was intriguing in itself.

But it turned out there was a whole lot of other facets to River Jack. Scientist. Warrior.

"You look surprised."

"I just didn't make the connection between jeweler and geologist. Maybe I should have." She scanned the framed artwork of gems and caves with new eyes, curiosity about him growing even as she learned more about him. "When did you retire from the service?"

A shadow crossed his face and she started to ask about his pain level, only to have him interrupt her.

"My wife had a health scare, and we decided to make the most of every moment." He scratched a thumb along the leather armrest. "I was at a point I could drop my retirement papers to leave the service. She recovered from the stage-two breast cancer, and lived for three more years. Then she died in a random car accident."

The tragedy of it hit her like a wave. Maybe because her emotions were still so close to the surface. Or perhaps because of the pain radiating off him. It was all just too sad, and she felt guilty for every moment she'd spent looking into his blue eyes.

She hugged a throw pillow to her stomach, hurting for him. "You must have loved her very much."

He nodded quietly, his throat moving with a slow swallow. "I'll be forever thankful for those last three years."

The devotion evident in his words said a lot about the kind of man he was.

And in spite of her resolve not to stare into his magnetic gaze or be drawn by his heartache, she felt a connection she hadn't experienced in a very long time. A prospect almost as frightening as her nightmares.

Chapter Ten

Sitting in a rocker by Lottie's bedside, Neve closed the third storybook in a row, this one about a mischievous puppy who went to service-dog school and made a wonderful new friend. The other tales had followed more of a festive theme with furry sidekicks saving Christmas or going on winter sledding adventures. The one with the mama dog who had a puppy for Christmas had almost made Neve teary, thinking about her own impending motherhood. It also made her treasure her time with her niece on a new level as she helped her with her bedtime ritual.

Lottie's room had been decorated for the holidays, even though they'd all been vigilant about encouraging the child to spend time in the family room as well. A pink artificial tree rested on top of the dresser, with tiny fairy lights. Miniature ornaments filled the limbs, all chosen by Lottie—a puppy, a horseshoe, a Santa, a child on a swing.

A manger scene was displayed at the base of the tree, a childlike version, with figurines made of plastic so she could handle them without fear of breaking.

There was even a little mismatched dog figure added beside the donkey. Behind it all, an Advent calendar with a piece of candy behind each number. Each night Lottie lobbied for an extra piece, just as Neve and her sisters had done growing up.

Glow-in-the-dark stars dotted the ceiling, and a holiday quilt covered the bed where Cocoa curled asleep on a comfy corner. Thankfully, Lottie had been able to keep her faithful companion close by. Often, exposure to pets was limited during the recovery, but the doctors had found the benefits of Cocoa's working presence far outweighed negligible risks.

Lottie tapped the final storybook. "Cocoa would get all A's at that school. She's the smartest, sweet-est, very best-est service dog ever. She even knows how to pull up the covers over me at night. Isn't that awesome?"

"Most awesome," Neve agreed, smoothing a hand along her niece's head and checking for fever. Lottie was cool, with no signs of swelling. Neve slid the purple, flowered water bottle to within reach on the bedside table. "Cocoa's being careful. She's a really good girl."

Lottie nodded, her hair in a braid to keep it from tangling. "She nudges me like that puppy in the story, when she knows I'm sad. So she's probably gonna wake up soon. Maybe you could take her outside for a potty break."

Sad?

Neve sat up straighter in the rocker, the three books

tumbling from her lap to the floor. Cocoa eased from the bed, careful not to jostle. The dog picked up a book in her mouth and set it back beside Lottie, then the other two as well before reclaiming her spot at the foot of the bed.

"What's wrong?" Neve asked, searching her face. "Should I get your mom?"

"Uh-uh. Mommy's taking a nap." Her face scrunched with worry. "I know she's really, really tired. I was up a lot last night."

Neve adjusted the quilt and patted her hand. "And do you need a rest too?"

"Maybe…" Lottie chewed her bottom lip, her eyes darting around the room.

Clearly, something was on the child's mind, but Neve wouldn't press just yet. Maybe if Lottie had more time, whatever was bothering her would bubble to the surface. "I'll stay here with you. We can listen to music, and if you get bored, we'll read again."

Neve cued Alexa with soft, instrumental Christmas tunes. She pressed a kiss to Lottie's forehead, then moved around the bedroom, gathering a pile of laundry from the top of the dresser to a laundry hamper. She stacked the pile of books they'd read together and moved them from the bed to a shelf in the nightstand.

Some of the stories were well-read, with tattered pages, others new, like the toys. Items from before their move to Moonlight Ridge mingled with more recent additions to make her recovery less tedious.

When Isobel and Cash had come to the Top Dog

Dude Ranch for the summer, they hadn't intended to stay. The pair hadn't even been a couple then, just friends. Neve and Zelda hadn't planned to stay either. But here they all still were, thanks to Gran's quest and the small inheritance she'd left with strict instructions to use it for their stay in Moonlight Ridge.

Isobel had stored the bulk of her furniture but brought her personal belongings into the cabin until she and Cash were ready to build a home of their own. Not that they would move far. They'd been scouting for land just outside the ranch's boundaries, well positioned for Cash's work at the resort and his volunteer firefighter duties.

Her sister's ability to pull up stakes like that and relocate still surprised Neve. It made her a little envious too. That big of a change felt overwhelming. Coming to Moonlight Ridge for this long had been tougher for her than her siblings seemed to realize. Zelda had embraced the new start, and Isobel simply said Lottie and Cash were her home.

But Neve had always enjoyed the comfort she took from having a firm sense of place. Her home was her nest, in a way, carefully built over time to reflect her life and her preferences so that she was surrounded by the things she loved. Was it superficial of her that she felt safe and comforted from the local barista knowing her coffee order or that she enjoyed taking care of her elderly neighbors' plants when they vacationed? Was it wrong to feel like she'd be tough to replace in her volunteer work at a local bird sanctuary?

In her mind's eye, she'd already envisioned bringing her child home there. To the nest she'd made special.

With the soft strains of violins playing "Silent Night," Neve tugged antibacterial wipes from a container and cleaned the doorknob, the light switch, and other surfaces in the already-spotless room. *Busy* was easier than *idle* with her worries knocking around in her mind.

"Aunt Neve," Lottie called out softly, "can I tell you a secret?"

Neve pivoted quickly and found her niece studying her with big, wide-awake eyes. "Of course, sweetie. But I want you to know you can also tell your mom anything. We wouldn't want to keep secrets from her."

"I know, but… I don't want her to be unhappy." A tear hovered, then spilled over. "I try hard to be brave, but I'm scared. I don't wanna be sick so much."

Neve's heart squeezed in her chest so hard it hurt. She'd never felt so powerless in her life. She just hoped her distress didn't show. "Your surgery went well. You know that, right? You're going to feel better soon. The doctors have every reason to believe you won't be sick so much once your body gets used to your new kidney."

Had she hit the right note in reassurance? She didn't want to mislead Lottie, but the answers weren't simple. And in fact, too much was unknown.

Another tear streaked down the child's cheek and onto the pillow. "Until the next time I get a problem because of my spina bifida. I gotta take medicine every day so my new kidney keeps working. What if my kidney is a reject?"

And there it was. The difficult truth that, of course, must be swirling in Lottie's mind, just as it did for Isobel and everyone else who cared about this sweet girl. Neve searched for the right words to tackle such a difficult conversation with a young child. She even considered waking Isobel up. Then an image of her sister's exhausted face came to mind.

"Lottie, I wish I had an easy answer for that." She could barely come to grips with the implications of her lupus diagnosis. Who was she to give out explanations? She settled for noting the only thing she felt in control of in her own medical world. "Your mama and Cash have made sure you have the best doctors to keep you healthy. They're smart, caring people, and they're all going to work hard to be sure you stay well."

Lottie fidgeted with her quilt, tracing the ornament patterns until the chocolate Labrador retriever inched forward to nudge her hand. "I just really don't wanna be sick at Christmas. It's not fair."

Agreed, little one. Agreed. Yet another point Neve was helpless to explain.

Neve wanted to offer to buy the moon, the stars, and anything else her niece might request, but Isobel had always been emphatic about not wanting Lottie to get spoiled. Isobel insisted that her daughter needed to understand the value of time spent with loved ones.

"Is there something you and I can do together to help make the holiday special?"

Lottie chewed her bottom lip thoughtfully, while stroking Cocoa's ear. Finally, her eyes lit. "I wanna play Candy Land five times. And, nobody can take out the cards that send you back to the start."

Smiling, Neve exhaled in relief. "That's a deal. And guess what? I hear there may be lots of other new board games under the tree for us to try out together."

There would also be a few more after she made a trip to the store. Surely Isobel could overlook a little extra spent on Lottie, especially when it came in the form of shared activities.

"Really? Ones that lots of people can play?" Her blue eyes danced with excitement for the first time since she woke up from surgery. "'Cause what I really want is for my whole family to be in the same place. That's what I wrote on the very top of my list to Santa, but don't tell anybody else because then my wish might not come true."

Neve's heart squeezed again, the girl's simple wish putting so much into perspective for her. Because truly, as much as Neve was attached to her home, she absolutely agreed that family came first and foremost.

"I'm sure that wish will definitely come true." Neve clasped Lottie's hand, appreciating the child's loving heart and sweet wisdom. "Being with my family is number one on my Christmas list too."

"Make sure Mr. Gil knows, too, so he can bring Mr.

River Jack," Lottie said, just before her face stretched with a huge yawn.

She covered her mouth and snuggled deeper into the covers. Cocoa scooched back to her corner at the end of the bed, apparently no longer worried about comforting her young charge.

As Neve watched her niece drift off to sleep, she felt grateful she'd been able to soothe some of her fears. Still, one aspect of their conversation continued to bother her. She'd told Lottie to trust her doctors and Neve had told herself she took comfort in that as well.

Except was it true? Had she truly listened to every detail of her medical care, especially during pregnancy? She certainly hoped so. But with the stakes so high and her health more precarious now, it was better to leave nothing to chance.

Once Lottie was fully asleep, Neve intended to pull out her cell phone. She needed to have a frank conversation with her obstetrician about possible pregnancy complications with an autoimmune disease. She didn't want to wait until her appointment in two days. She needed to know now, so she would be ready for an informed conversation when she spoke to Gil.

Gil didn't know how he would have managed to juggle work and his father's early recovery at home without the help of the nurse. While his dad was not fully healed by any means, Gil could breathe a little easier. Enough so, he decided to stop by Lottie's on his way to his father's for the night.

Knocking on the door with one hand, he juggled his grip on the bag of gifts he'd brought for the young patient. He couldn't deny he hoped to cross paths with Neve too. There'd been no time to see each other since Lottie and River Jack were released from the hospital. They'd only communicated by a few brief text messages. And with each day that passed, he was all too aware of her impending departure.

The door swung open…to reveal Cash. Gil tried not to let his smile falter. "I hope I'm not intruding. I just brought a little something for Lottie."

"Please, come in." Cash motioned him through the door.

As Gil stepped inside, he saw the full family room. Zelda, Troy, and Harper, along with Isobel holding Lottie with Cocoa at their feet. And thank heaven, Neve sat by the fire, with her feet tucked under her.

His smile widened.

He lifted the bright bag with tissue paper sticking out. "Hello, Lottie. I have a special delivery present just for you."

Squealing, Lottie clapped her hands. "But it's not Christmas yet."

"This is a get-well gift." Gil set the sack on the coffee table, all too aware of Neve's gaze lingering on him. "Your Christmas one will be under the tree."

Lottie reached for the bag patterned with a unicorn leading a sleigh. "The wrapping is so pretty. My mommy saves the wrapping and I'm gonna ask her to put one of my presents in this one every year."

Laughing, Isobel shifted her daughter onto the sofa and sat beside her, before setting the present between them.

Lottie flung aside the tissue paper, one piece after another. Gasping in delight, she pulled out a box with multiple games. "A tic-tac-toe board, and checkers, and dice. Thank you, thank you."

"Keep looking," he urged, smiling at her obvious delight. Her color was good and she moved around well considering her recent surgery. Both things so reassuring.

She fished deeper into the bag and withdrew different decks of cards.

Isobel grinned up at him before pointing to each deck as she explained them to Lottie. "This one's a game called Uno. And here's Go Fish with all sorts of colorful, hand-painted fish on them. And this one's Crazy Eights. We'll have such fun playing with them together."

Lottie hugged the box to her chest, excitement glowing. "I was just telling Aunt Neve that I wanted more games for Christmas."

"And she told me." He scooped up the paper and knelt by the fire. Near Neve. "So I thought part of the holidays could come a little early." One at a time, he tossed the wadded paper into the fireplace, the flames arcing higher.

Neve's gaze met his and held, the noise in the room fading for a moment. He wanted to reach for her, to hold her hand. But that would broadcast their relationship, when they'd both insisted on waiting. The time to talk to their families was drawing near.

Would they be able to explore their relationship more openly then?

"Mommy," Lottie's voice pierced the fog. "What's auto-mune?"

Gil frowned.

And Neve froze.

Isobel tipped her head to the side. "Auto-mune?"

"Yeah, auto-mune." Lottie nodded. "Is it a sick car?"

"A sick car?" Gil leaned forward, elbows on his knees... Then realization dawned. "Like an autoimmune disease?"

"Yeah, that." Lottie snapped her fingers. Well, sort of snapped, in a soft, childlike motion.

Isobel set aside the games and patted her daughter's hand. "Why do you want to know?"

"Aunt Neve was talking on the phone about auto-mune stuff," Lottie explained earnestly. "She thought I was sleeping, but I was listening 'cause I was bored. Does that make me a very bad girl, Mommy?"

"You're a wonderful young lady," Isobel said. "The very best daughter."

A prickling sense of realization crept up his spine, a feeling compounded by all of the confused gazes darting from Lottie to Neve and back again.

Lottie put her hands on either side of her mother's face. "Mommy, can Aunt Neve stay here with me more while I get better? We can keep each other company since she's got auto-mune sickness. I heard her talking to her doctor all about it."

Isobel frowned in confusion.

A queasy feeling settled in Gil's gut while chatter between mother and daughter filled the awkward silence. Maybe the kid misunderstood? But somehow, he didn't think so. It was too specific a word for her to have manufactured on her own.

The stricken look on Neve's face wasn't reassuring in the least.

The sick feeling in his gut increased. What kind of autoimmune disease did Neve have? And what implications would that have for her and the baby? Important questions.

And they were questions he intended to find out the answers to as soon as he could get a private minute with the mother of his child.

Neve felt like the rug had been yanked out from under her.

She'd been so sure Lottie was sleeping during the phone conversation. Neve hadn't wanted to step away into the hall for her call, afraid to take her eyes off her niece for even a moment.

But there was no way around it. The whole room full of family—and Gil—now knew that she had an autoimmune disease and that she hadn't told anyone.

Neve shrugged, scrunching her nose in chagrin. "Well, the secret's out. I was diagnosed, uh, recently—" she fudged the truth ever so slightly "—with lupus."

She watched Gil out of the corner of her eyes, only to find his face inscrutable. She knew him well enough to realize he wouldn't press the point in front of the others, so she concentrated on giving the rest of the family the answers they needed.

Neve focused on Lottie, needing to fix this with her before anyone else since that overheard conversation had given the child one more thing to feel anxious about. "But I don't want you to worry. I know *lupus* is a strange word."

Lottie frowned. "Will you have it forever or will medicine make you better?"

"I will have it forever." She settled for a simple, but truthful, explanation. "But that doesn't mean I will feel sick all the time. Far from it. I just have to be extracareful not to get tired because if I get worn down and sick, it will take me longer to get better."

Nodding, Lottie said, "I'm sorry that happened to you, but I'm glad you have good doctors."

Hearing the child echo words from their conversation touched her heart and she breathed a sigh of relief. "That's right. I have a smart team of physicians to look after me, and they will make sure I stay as healthy as I can be."

She hoped her words would remind Lottie that she was in good hands too.

Lottie fidgeted on the sofa. "Cash, can I have some tablet time? I'm getting tired and I need to be careful—like Aunt Neve."

Cash shot to his feet. "Hey kiddo, how about we go to the sunroom?"

Troy stood as well, tucking the games back into the gift bag. "Harper and I will come, too, and we could play Uno, if you'd rather that instead of your tablet."

Cheering, Lottie extended her arms to be carried. "Yay! I definitely wanna play Uno first."

Once the room cleared out to just her sisters and silent Gil, Neve folded her arms over her chest. "So, what questions do you have?"

Isobel's face creased with worry, a hint of hurt. "Why didn't you tell us?"

Neve searched for the right words. "You had plenty on your plate with the search for a kidney donor, and then the surgery. My health care team and I have everything under control."

During the call today, her doctor's nurse answered questions and added an extra twenty minutes to the upcoming appointment with the obstetrician to discuss any further concerns.

Isobel leaned forward to clasp Neve's hands. "But I want to support you."

Zelda toyed with the tail of her braid. "Sometimes it's difficult to tell the people you love your biggest hurts. Like how I struggled to share about my time in Atlanta with my ex-boyfriend."

Isobel winced. "I'm so sorry. I didn't mean to be insensitive to either of you."

Zelda waved away the concern. "Thank you, but

that's in my past. Right now, this moment is about Neve. Please, tell us more about your diagnosis."

More than anything, Neve wanted to go back in time when they weren't looking at her with such sympathy and concern. "I'm lucky my doctor got the diagnosis so quickly. Many people with lupus go undiagnosed for years, decades even, just chasing the symptoms. I'm fine. I promise."

Isobel squeezed her hands. "No more secrets, okay?"

Neve stifled a wince as she thought of her pregnancy. But she and Gil had a plan on when to share the news and they needed to keep the timing for meeting with his father in mind. That was her reason for delaying.

Not because she wanted to delay the questions from her sisters about Gil for as long as possible. Questions she didn't have a clue how to answer.

Besides, right now wasn't the time to launch into more discussion of her health with her sisters. Gil deserved an explanation first. She owed him her focus, along with the quiet and freedom to discuss her secrecy about her lupus diagnosis. "I'm going to head on back to my cabin. I need to let Rudy out." She pivoted toward Gil. "Would you mind walking me home?"

Gil rose from sitting on the edge of the stone hearth and extended a hand. "Of course. Dad's nurse has another hour on her shift."

The goodbyes to her sisters passed in a blur, nerves making her jittery with regret. She'd handled this poorly, and for a person who prided herself on making smart, measured choices, falling short stung. She should have told him sooner but she'd been so afraid he would look at her differently, treat her differently.

Once outside, the bracing winter air cleared her mind. The stars had just started to twinkle through the trees, brighter up in the mountains without the dilution of smog. The soft echo of music from the direction of one of the barns hinted at a party underway. As Lottie had said, Neve wished this could be a simpler holiday, where they were all free to celebrate in simple ways, together, with no weighty concerns hanging over them like heavy storm clouds.

Each breath icy and crisp in her lungs, she paused on Isobel's porch to tug on her gloves and waited for his response. And she didn't have to wait long.

His jaw was tensed and his hands stuffed in his coat pockets. "When were you going to tell me about your autoimmune disease?" His voice stayed low and even. "Or did you plan for the doctor to just drop the bombshell in my lap at the appointment? You have to know I'm...upset."

And in that moment, she realized he wasn't angry. He was hurt.

Defensiveness melted away and she touched his arm lightly, his weatherproof parka crinkling under her fingertips. "I know it may be tough for you to believe me, but I fully intended to tell you before the appointment."

He looked down, scuffing the toe of his work boots

along the salted porch. "I don't have any choice but to accept your word."

Starch crept back up her spine. "Do you realize I'm not obligated to tell you any of it?"

His gaze shifted back up to meet hers, full of vulnerability. "I thought we were moving beyond that superficial fling to something deeper that could help us co-parent our child. Maybe even learning how to trust each other to put the needs of our child before our own."

His words made her bristle, yet she couldn't deny he had a point.

"You're right," she conceded, unable to deny the attraction had shifted into something more these past few weeks. Something more substantive and confusing. "I just need for you to know that I wouldn't do anything to put this pregnancy at risk."

A gasp echoed from behind her and she pivoted fast to find the front door open, releasing a gust of warm air. Her sisters stood side by side, gaping.

Isobel stepped onto the porch, hugging her sweater tighter around herself. Her eyes went wide with surprise. "You're having a baby?"

Chapter Eleven

"You're having a baby?" Isobel repeated, her shocked words puffing small white clouds into the cold air. "Did I hear you right?"

Zelda peeked over her shoulder, braid swinging forward. "What's going on? Are you pregnant?"

Wincing, Neve stole a quick look at Gil, who was scrubbing a hand across his face. She'd barely recovered from everyone accidentally discovering about her autoimmune diagnosis. And now, all her plans for sharing her baby news in a controlled manner...?

Poof.

Up in smoke.

She struggled for the right words. Should they place a quick FaceTime call to River Jack so he would be in on the belated reveal? Or just forge ahead with her sisters, then speak with him afterward?

None of it felt right. And worse, the slipup with the baby news had robbed her of the chance to really smooth things over with Gil about her lupus. She had only just begun to gather her thoughts about that, and now? She would have whiplash after today.

Gil palmed her back. "Let's go inside and talk before we all turn into popsicles."

Thank heaven he'd taken the lead so she wouldn't have to feel guilty about his father finding out second instead of their original plan. Well, given all the people in the cabin, he would be finding out…seventh?

Following her sisters, Gil ushered Neve inside the warmth of the cabin, where Cash was dealing Uno cards to Troy, Lottie, and Harper. "Neve? Do you want to tell them?"

Meeting Gil's gaze briefly, she understood that he was resigned to sharing the news sooner rather than later. Funny how she could read those thoughts just by looking into his eyes. When had that connection developed between them?

She drew in a bracing breath, just as if she was diving off a high cliff. There would be no turning around after this. "I'm having a baby and Gil is the father."

Squeals and cheers filled the cabin. Joy shone on all the faces around them. Her family's exuberant response to the news reminded her how monumental it was. They were having a baby. And while Neve already loved her child, so very much, for the first time, she felt…deeply excited and celebrated rather than nervous and scared.

Questions and felicitations twined together so tightly it was tough to tell who said what as the room erupted into spontaneous questions and comments…

"How far along are you?"

"When did you find out?"

"Congrats, man."

"I'm gonna be a cousin."

"What great news."

"Welcome to the family, Gil."

That last one stopped her short and she avoided his eyes. Technically, there hadn't been a question about marriage, but the implication hung in the air all the same.

The cheers melted into an awkward silence for a handful of heartbeats before Isobel clapped her hands.

"Okay, this calls for a toast. I bought sparkling grape juice for Christmas and now seems the perfect time to open it." Isobel called over her shoulder, "Neve? Zelda? Come help me carry everything."

Well, wasn't that an obvious ploy to get her away for questions? But she might as well surrender. She would do the same thing if the situations were reversed.

Isobel tugged open a cabinet and pulled down wine glasses before turning to the refrigerator. "I can't wait to spoil my little niece or nephew."

Zelda pulled a bamboo tray from the top of the microwave and began arranging the glasses. "How long have you known about the baby?"

"Not long. Around three months." Neve hedged. "I wasn't keeping it a secret exactly. I just wanted to wait awhile before going public."

Isobel set the bottle on the tray and booted the refrigerator door closed. "The news is yours to share when you're ready. There's no pressure from me—

and my lips will be sealed. How does Gil feel about the baby? He was quiet during your announcement."

"He's as stunned...and excited as I am." She would make sure her child always felt welcomed and wanted. And most of all, loved. For all the worries she'd had about her health, about how to co-parent and where to live, she'd never once questioned how she felt about having a baby.

Zelda smiled as she added a small stack of napkins. "That's good to hear. And just what I would expect from what I've seen of him these past months. He's a great guy."

Might as well get past the inevitable question. Sighing, she leaned back against the counter. "Aren't you going to ask what our plans are?"

Isobel thumbed a spot off a glass. "I figure you'll tell me when you're ready. I'm guessing we've probably pried out enough secrets regarding your personal life today."

"That's kind of you, but truth be told," Neve said, nerves fluttering, "we don't have plans right now, beyond giving ourselves some breathing room to absorb the news."

And while six months sounded like a long time to restructure her life, the days were flying by at an alarming rate.

Zelda slid an arm around her shoulders. "I know this is probably jumping the gun. But have you picked out any names?"

In quiet moments, in the far reaches of her heart.

Yes. She had dreamed of what to call her child. When she wasn't scared to death. "If it's a girl, I was thinking Alice, for Gran, and call her Allie."

Isobel's hand trembled as she covered her mouth. "That's absolutely beautiful. I should have thought of it when my Lottie was born. And if it's a boy?"

"I don't know yet." Because she just had a gut feeling the baby was a girl, but it felt silly—unscientific—to say that. "I've been scouring baby-name sites online, but no luck. It's still early yet. Although spinning Alice into Allister does have a cool vintage vibe."

"Allister?" Zelda quirked an eyebrow. "Gil will want to have a say about that."

They shared a good-natured laugh, and Neve welcomed the lightheartedness, the familiar connection with her sisters after the past three months of worry. Gran's will had brought them back together in Moonlight Ridge after they'd let their sibling bond lapse. Isobel coming from out West. Zelda leaving the seclusion of her possessive ex-boyfriend behind in Atlanta. And of course, Neve had thrown herself into her career, a field of study that still brought her such immense satisfaction.

Isobel chewed her bottom lip, eyebrows pulling together. "I wouldn't want to pressure you," she said cautiously, "but have you thought about staying here? Or will he be moving to North Carolina with you?"

Neve fought back the urge to snap at her sister, the question too like one Gil had asked her. She'd gone through so much change to her orderly world these past few months. She couldn't wrap her brain around any more, and she was running out of ways to explain herself to all the free spirits around her. "Right now, we're just focused on an uneventful pregnancy and a healthy baby."

Zelda's eyes went wide. "Oh my," she gasped. "I didn't even think about your autoimmune disease."

Isobel's face creased with concern. "How are you feeling? Are there any risk factors for you?"

Her skin prickled and she hated the defensiveness creeping over her. She wanted the joy back when her sisters had squealed on the porch. "Can we talk about that another time?" She lifted the tray from the counter. "Right now, I just want to celebrate that I'm going to be a mom and the two of you are going to be the most amazing aunts ever."

Gil prided himself on being a go-with-the-flow kind of guy, a trait that served him well in his job where the unexpected could happen at any moment. Equipment breaking during a climbing outing. A guest losing an oar right before they went over some rapids when he took a group whitewater rafting. He was an expert at problem-solving on the fly.

But at the moment, he was struggling to find his balance after the surprise baby-news reveal earlier. No question, he was the one without an oar, and he didn't have a clue how to paddle. He should have realized they couldn't keep a secret around this place for long.

Now, after toasting the pregnancy with her sisters,

he and Neve were in his dad's driveway for round two of sharing the baby news. This time, in a more controlled fashion. Isobel had even sent an extra bottle of sparkling grape juice with them for more toasting.

Except the woman in the passenger seat looked far from festive. Her forehead was scrunched about as tightly as his nervous gut. He and Neve hadn't spoken during the drive over beyond simple exchanges...

Are you warm enough?

Is the music too loud?

Did River Jack respond to your text telling him we're coming over?

Shifting the truck into Park, Gil turned toward her, leather upholstery creaking as he wished he could do something to ease her nerves. "Are you ready? Dad's expecting us."

Finally, she looked at him full on, her eyes full of wariness in the dash lights. "I'm so sorry to have wrecked the plans for how we would tell our families."

"And you wanted to wait until after the doctor visit." He took her hand in his, needing her to understand that he didn't blame her for a second about the baby news getting out early. If they were going to parent together, they would have to start backing each other up. Support one another. "Plans don't always go smoothly."

"We're a testament to that."

"Thank you for coming with me this evening. I know it's been a long day, but I didn't want to risk my dad finding out from someone else."

"It's the right thing to do." She squeezed his fingers. "Now, let's get moving."

He pressed a kiss to her mouth, not lingering, just a quick brush of his lips against hers before skirting the trunk to open her door. The outdoor staircase that he'd raced up countless times growing up now gave him pause when he thought of Neve climbing it. Such a simple thing, but his world had shifted on its axis these past weeks.

He braced a palm low on her back, even though he'd salted the steps that morning for the nurse, in case the predicted ice storm started early. Weather was unpredictable this time of year and already this had been a harsh winter.

Before he could reach for the knob, Priscilla pulled open the door, the wreath jingling.

"Welcome," she said. "Your dad will be glad to have the extra company. He's been chomping at the bit with boredom all day."

Gil took Neve's lined coat and hung it alongside his own on the iron coat tree. "Sorry to hear our patient has been giving you grief," he said before walking deeper into the living room where his father reclined in his favorite leather chair. "Priscilla, would you mind getting four glasses? We've got news to celebrate."

Neve held up the bottle of sparkling grape juice. "It's still cold. Nonalcoholic since you're recovering from surgery and..."

Gil grinned and hope it didn't look too forced.

"...because Neve and I are excited to tell you that we're expecting."

Stunned silence echoed, broken only by the pop and hiss of burning logs in the fireplace. The settling log snapped the tension.

River Jack clapped a hand over his heart. "A grandfather? Now, isn't that the best Christmas present ever? Better than anything under the tree for certain." He nodded toward the towering pine, strung only with lights. "Congratulations, you two."

"Thanks, Dad."

Priscilla backed toward the kitchen. "I'll get those glasses. Best wishes to you both. And to River Jack as well."

Gil motioned to the sofa for Neve to sit, then joined her. "Dad, I know this news comes as a surprise—"

"A welcome surprise," River Jack interrupted, looking pleased, if a bit pale.

Had he overexerted himself?

"Very," Neve said, glowing with a happiness that took Gil's breath away.

He had to tug his focus off her and back to his father. "This pregnancy wasn't planned, but we both want the baby. Very much. I want to be clear, though, that while we're not a couple, we're committed to co-parenting."

River Jack's gaze skipped back and forth between them as if he wanted to ask more. Then he simply nodded. "Well, this child will get unlimited love from his or her granddaddy. You can plan on that."

"All the more motivation for you to take care of yourself and follow the doctor's orders." He turned to Priscilla as she returned with four champagne flutes. "Is he being a compliant patient?"

She placed the glasses on the coffee table, along with a stack of napkins. "For the most part."

River Jack shrugged, followed by a wince. "I want to move around more, but she insists I'm trying to push myself too fast."

"My vote," Gil said as he opened the sparkling grape juice, "is trust the lady with the nursing degree."

Neve held up one glass after another to be filled. "Put your feet up. Watch a Christmas movie."

Quirking an eyebrow, Priscilla took her glass. "We've already seen *Die Hard*. Twice."

River Jack clapped a hand to his chest. "Don't disrespect the classic."

Priscilla rolled her eyes. "Right up there with *It's a Wonderful Life*."

Grinning, Neve lifted her drink, bubbles sparkling to the surface. "Before your next shift, I'll text River Jack some recommendations that may have a broader appeal."

Gil started to breathe easier, the announcement having gone smoother than he'd expected, with fewer questions. For whatever reason, his dad was giving him the space he needed as he sorted out the relationship with Neve.

The toasting and chitchat passed in a haze, much like with Neve's family, and he realized he'd been running on adrenaline since he learned he would be a dad. And then holding strong through his father's surgery. The revelation that Neve had an autoimmune condition to worry about had thrown him for a loop, too, but she had assured him she was doing everything her care team recommended for a healthy pregnancy.

Although, he could swear he finally felt the tension inside start to ease. He had hope that he could sort through matters with Neve, that they could find a less complicated path into the future.

Conversation flowed around him with an effortlessness he hadn't expected, due in large part to Priscilla. The nurse checked his dad's vitals and refilled glasses without disrupting the flow of the get-together. So much so, he'd lost track of the passing of time.

Setting his emptied glass on the table, he said, "I need to get Neve back to her cabin before the ice storm starts. Priscilla, are you okay to stay for another hour while I take Neve home?"

"Of course," she answered without hesitation. "We were just going to eat supper before you arrived. I made whole wheat bread to go with chicken-vegetable stew. There's plenty for when you get back."

"You've been a lifesaver." Standing, he pointed to his father. "Be nice to that nurse. I like her."

After a handful more congratulatory hugs, Gil passed Neve her coat and shrugged into his own. Once they picked their way down the stairs and settled into the truck, Gil cranked the heater on full blast and sagged back in his seat. "Whew, I don't know about you, but that wiped me out."

She released a long, exhausted-sounding exhale. "That was a lot of emotion for one evening. But it went well. Your dad seems genuinely happy."

His gaze zeroed back in on his childhood home with the tree glowing in the window. His father and mother had always dreamed of being grandparents someday. The thought brought a pinch of loss. "Yeah, he sure did. I imagine he's probably got his nurse looking up kiddie holiday movies as we speak."

Neve clicked her seatbelt, then wiggled her hands in front of the heater vents. "Do you think River Jack and Priscilla are an item?"

"My dad?" Shock speared him, followed by denial. "Nah. Just because we kept our relationship a secret must have you imagining things. Dad would have told me."

"I don't know. Seemed to me there were sparks flying when they talked. And I could swear your father's eyes followed her wherever she went."

"I didn't notice." He put the truck into Drive and steered out of the circular driveway, gravel crunching under the tires. Mountains and the dense forest blocked most of the moonlight, and he clicked on the high beams.

"How would you feel about it?" She shifted in the seat toward him. "If they started dating? Has your father gone out with anyone since your mom passed away?"

His mouth went dry and he swallowed twice. Of course he wanted his dad to be happy. "He hasn't seen anyone, that I know of. As for how I would feel? I want my father to enjoy life. I recognize it might seem strange at first, but he has decades ahead of him."

"Good," she said, a knowing smile on her face. "I'm glad to hear that."

He held up a hand. "But I still don't think you're right."

"Okay, then."

Her smile turned into a laugh that filled the truck cab, almost easing the renewed tension knotting his gut as the first pellets of sleek pinged the windshield.

Priscilla had tended numerous patients over the years and kept her professionalism firmly in place. All jokes about movie choices aside, River Jack had been a fairly compliant patient. Sure, he got restless and bored, but who wouldn't? And at times, he was downright charming.

Plus, this evening felt warm and easy, almost familial. And that shouldn't be happening. No question, she was growing too comfortable here, and her years as a soldier had taught her that letting down her guard could be dangerous.

She waited for him to right his electric recliner before placing his dinner on the wooden TV tray in front of him, the sound of the icy precipitation drumming against the windows. "Looks like that ice storm isn't going to let up anytime soon. Thank goodness

Gil and Neve made it safely to her cabin before the worst of it started."

"Sorry you're stuck here for the night," he called as she walked back to the kitchen to get her dinner.

"I'm just glad it started before I left, rather than when I was already on the road." She placed her meal on the coffee table before sitting cross-legged on the sofa. "When the baby comes, what name will you want to be called? Grandpa? Grandaddy?"

"I'm not sure. It's all still pretty new." He dipped his whole-grain bread into the stew and bit off the corner.

"What did you call your grandfathers?" She placed her tray on her lap.

"Pop Pop and Bubba."

She scrunched her nose. "I can't see you as either of those."

His eyes twinkled even as they narrowed. "Is that a compliment or insult?"

She laughed but didn't answer.

He spooned up a taste of the stew and *hmm*ed in appreciation. "That's heartier than I expected. To be honest, I expected bland and unpalatable. I figured I would just eat a little politely, then find something else to chow down on once Gil took over for the evening. But this is amazing. You've sure got a way with spices."

She looked up sharply. Was it her imagination or had he lingered over the word *spices*, before the air turned awkward? Surely not, especially in his current state.

"I'm glad you're enjoying it. Eat up."

He set his spoon in the bowl. "What about you? Any kids? Grandchildren?"

"Nope," she said. The sting of regret had her reaching for her water glass. "One divorce. No children."

Thankfully, he didn't press for more. He just swallowed down another bite, stirring the spoon in his bowl. "I think I would want to be called Papa Jack."

"I like that," she said. "It fits."

"Certainly better than Old Man River."

They shared an easy laugh, eating half of their meal while holiday tunes echoed softly from the sound system. "O Holy Night" gave way to "It Came Upon a Midnight Clear."

She dabbed at the corner of her mouth. "Sorry you're having a quieter Christmas this year."

"I'm fine. You're the one who's having to work over the holidays. Maybe I'll surprise everyone and be back up to speed sooner than expected."

She set aside her napkin and moved her tray back to the coffee table. "I don't mind either way. Sometimes I have come to appreciate other people's holiday traditions while I'm working. One of my most vivid Christmas memories happened when I was deployed. Everyone who received cookies or candies from home shared them. I can still taste these fruitcake cookies. Since then, I've tried to recreate the recipe each year and they never measure up."

"I suppose Christmas cookies are off the menu for my recovery," he half groused.

"Moderation is key." She logged a mental note to cook gingerbread with the next meal and refused to linger overlong on why the thought made her heart beat faster. Seeing he'd finished his meal, she moved his tray to the coffee table. "What's one of your favorite holiday memories?"

He scratched his chin thoughtfully, his gaze tracking her. "We had all sorts of expectations for our first Christmas with Gil. We filled the house with decorations and strung lights on all the bushes outside. I even climbed up on the roof to put a plastic Santa by the chimney. My wife just about bought out the toy store."

"Of course you were both excited." She settled back on the sofa, hugging a throw pillow and picking at the fringed piping. "It must have been a magical time."

He shook his head wryly. "Quite frankly, it was overwhelming for Gil. He shut down and wouldn't talk for the longest time."

"What did you do?"

"We waited. And wondered. And worried as December the twenty-fifth grew closer." His eyes took on a faraway look as he stared out the picture window, sleet clicking softly outside. "Finally, one day in the McDonald's drive-through, he asked for a Christmas chicken."

"A Christmas chicken?"

"We were just as confused as you look right now," he said with a fond smile. "Apparently, his biological mom didn't make a full turkey. Instead, she baked a chicken. I don't know if she chose that for financial reasons or simply to be more practical for two people eating. But it made me realize we'd put our expectations for the holiday on to him, rather than figuring out what felt familiar to a child who'd just faced such a massive change."

The memory was so sweet her chest went tight, thinking of the three of them finding their way to becoming a family here in this house. "That's very insightful."

"We lucked into the answer. Then we took down all the decorations while he was at kindergarten. When we picked him up, we went to the store and had him show us what Christmas decorations he liked best."

"What did he choose?"

"A little tabletop tree, the kind with frosted-white needles." He gripped the arms of his recliner with a sigh. "He asked to go sledding. That trek down the hill started my quest to tap into every outdoor activity available to do with him so we could bond."

And now Gil Hadley had turned those memories into a career. Yet another way this man had built an amazing life in this perfect house. She envied him that special family, but at the same time accepted that, after the horrors she'd seen, she wasn't anywhere close to the kind of person who would have fit into this fairy-tale world.

Chapter Twelve

When Neve had told Gil they needed to spend more time together, she hadn't meant for them to be stranded in her cabin during an ice storm. But there was no denying that the roads weren't safe tonight. With temperatures still dropping, she didn't expect the situation to change before morning, at the earliest.

Her quaint log cottage narrowed with intimacy. From the flames snapping and popping in the fireplace to the warm glow of the tree lights. She knelt in front of Rudy to tug on his bright red sweater and booties as Gil stacked the last plate in the dishwasher. He'd insisted, since she had cooked.

If grilled peanut-butter-and-jelly sandwiches could be called cooking.

But they were her latest craving and he'd been game to try them. Served with a glass of milk. She couldn't get enough of them.

Or of him.

"Hey," Gil called out, drying his hands on a kitchen towel. "Let me take care of Rudy. I salted those steps while you were cooking, but it's still slippery and the sleet's coming down fast. You don't have to be out here."

Thinking of the frigid weather outdoors, she didn't need convincing. "Thanks. You won't find me begging to freeze out there."

His palm grazed her back as he passed to scoop up the puppy. "Come on, Rudy, boy. Let's see how well you play fetch with icy chunks."

The beagle pup licked his chin, their bond already strong. Seeing his ease with the little fella made her heart swell. He would be an attentive father. And fun.

She watched them through the window as he sprinted around the yard, half skating on his boots some of the time, but effectively running out the puppy's energy. His zest for life drew her, even as she knew she would be hard-pressed to keep up with Gil's seemingly endless energy. How easy it was to envision him with their child and a grown Rudy, playing and making memories together.

Her phone buzzed in her pocket, snapping her from her musings. She tugged her cell free to find that... Zelda was FaceTiming.

Neve accepted the call. "What's going on?" Nerves kicked in as she wondered... "Is something wrong with Lottie?"

"No, not at all," Zelda assured her from a rocker, the Christmas tree twinkling behind her. "She's sleeping comfortably. I just saw that you two made it back safely. If you need anything tonight when Gil goes back to his father's just let us know."

Neve leaned against the window, parted curtain clutched in her hand. "Um, Gil decided to stay." So much for convincing her family they weren't a couple. "His dad's nurse couldn't leave because of the roads. We decided it's safest for everyone to stay put."

"Interesting." Her sister's blue eyes lit with a knowing glimmer. "Is he in the room with you now?"

"He's outside with the puppy." Neve turned the phone orientation to show him outside in the glow of the security light, tossing chunks of ice for Rudy to pounce upon. Then flipped the image back to her own face. "You wouldn't guess how cold it is, watching them playing."

"I'll definitely leave the two of you alone, then." A mischievous twinkle lit her blue eyes. "You're going to need to dry your clothes and snuggle to conserve body heat."

"Zelda, we meant it when we said we aren't a couple." The words sounded weak, even to herself.

Her sister laughed. "Well, you clearly were a couple at some point about a few months ago, even if the rest of the world didn't know. Maybe you can recapture that feeling."

Feelings weren't the problem. In fact, there were far too many of them coursing through her. "Things are more complicated now, with the baby."

"I can empathize with that." Zelda shifted her fluffy Maltese mix in her lap, hugging her closer. "Troy and I have had to consider his daughter's feelings and keep her well-being at the forefront. Teenage dynamics are no walk in the park."

"From the outside, Harper seems really happy, so it seems like you're doing a great job managing," Neve rushed to assure her.

"And so will you. Trust yourself and your feelings. Enjoy this time alone with Gil," Zelda said firmly. "I need to run. Troy made us chili and fried cornbread for supper. Don't hesitate to phone me if you need anything. Bye, now."

The call disconnected and Neve clutched the cell to her chest as she stared out at Gil without watchful eyes on her. He gathered up Rudy in careful arms and started back toward the cabin, his gaze locking with hers. He smiled. Just a simple grin, but warmth spread through her, like spiked cider. She wanted to attribute the feeling to her sister's words about being a couple.

Yet Neve knew better. The attraction to Gil was only getting stronger with time. If that was even possible.

The front door swung open, letting a blast of cold air inside. Pellets of ice clung to his hair and shoulders, his cheeks reddened from the wind.

She set her phone aside and reached for the puppy. "Let me have him while you warm up."

His arm skimmed against her chest as he transferred Rudy to her. "It wasn't that cold. It was invigorating, actually. And just what I needed to burn off the tension from those two family meetings."

Sitting on the floor in front of the fire, she peeled

off Rudy's sweater and booties, the little fella squirming to get free. She set the damp doggie gear along the hearth to dry. "The pair of you seemed to have fun out there."

He shrugged out of his coat and brushed the moisture from his sandy-brown hair before sitting on the edge of the hearth, his back to the fire as he untied his work boots. "I'm happiest when I'm outdoors."

"Even when it's sleeting?" Without thinking, she picked at pellets of ice stuck to the leg of his jeans. Muscles twitched under her touch.

The room went silent and still as awareness charged the air.

"Even then." He lifted a lock of her hair and tugged ever so lightly before tucking the strand behind her ear. "This little guy ups the fun factor."

"I have to admit I'm relieved no one has stepped up to claim him." Even as they spoke back and forth, she knew the words were just blanketing the undercurrent between them. The desire crackled as tangibly as the fire.

"Neve…" His voice came out hoarse with a need echoed inside her. "I'm trying my best to keep my distance, but make no mistake, I want you. I have since the moment I laid eyes on you."

"I know," she said breathlessly, trying her best not to sway into him.

"You were the one who wanted distance, rather than continuing our…"

"Fling." The word itself explained why they couldn't continue.

She'd understood from the start that he was the epitome of rootless bachelor. Did she want more? Had she pushed him away out of self-preservation? Valid questions she should have realized before, back when she only needed to worry about herself. But the baby had to come first. A child due in a few months.

A child that wasn't here yet.

Would it be so wrong to steal a few more memories with Gil before she left Moonlight Ridge for good? What harm could there be in indulging the need inside her, as long as she made her stance clear? "Could we do that? Just have a final fling before I leave?"

"Is that what you want?" He shifted from the hearth to the floor beside her, cradling her face in his hand. "I need for us both to be certain, because of the future we'll share."

"You wanted us to use this holiday season to explore how to navigate our relationship." She rose up onto her knees and slid her arms around his neck, pressing her breasts to his chest. The spicy scent of him filled her senses, but then, when hadn't he filled her thoughts? As tantalizing as when he filled her body.

Her mouth was a mere whisper away from his. "And right now, I want to *explore* every inch of your body."

The next morning, Gil cranked his truck heater on high, throwing the vehicle into four-wheel drive. He hadn't wanted to leave the warmth of sharing Neve's bed, with her skin silky against him. But she'd been sleeping so soundly and the pup needed to be let out. So he'd hauled himself from under the quilt, carefully.

The second his feet had hit the freezing floor, he'd realized there'd been a power outage. If he'd been a guest at the ranch, he would have crawled right back under those covers. But as an employee, he'd needed to check in with his boss to see how far the outage had spread.

Luckily, the ranch had taken precautions to ensure their guests stayed toasty warm. Each cabin had a generator that ran on a timer for a certain amount of hours each day, when needed, just enough to keep the pipes from freezing.

Still, he and Jacob were delivering extra firewood to the cabins to supplement heat.

Jacob tipped back his YETI full of steaming java. "I appreciate how fast you came over to help out today, checking on guests and delivering firewood."

"Of course, that's all a part of the job. You know how much I enjoy working here," Gil answered, reaching for his own thermos as he steered slowly along the icy roads. He'd left breakfast on the bedside table for Neve, a couple of pastries and a thermos of hot tea, along with a note telling her where he'd gone.

And that he *would* check in at lunchtime.

He didn't want her doubting for a minute that he would be back. Their lovemaking had been even more intense than before, no doubt in part because of the stakes and knowing that, regardless, they were connected forever now.

Would she understand that things didn't have to be so complicated? Why couldn't they continue on as they had? Certainly, the more time they spent together, the more he realized how much she meant to him.

Hopefully, she would come to feel the same. He'd even brought Rudy along so the pup wouldn't wake her. The beagle was curled up on the bench seat between him and Jacob, enjoying ear scratches at every stop along the way.

Pulling up in front of their fifth cabin stop of the day, he recognized three of the Purl Girls bundled up on the porch waiting. He threw the truck into Park, picked up Rudy, and hopped out. "Good morning, ladies. Do you mind if I let my puppy run around in your fenced yard while we unload firewood?"

The trio picked their way down the steps. Veronica, the leader of their pack, clapped her gloved hands. "We would love that. We'll keep him occupied. Won't we, sweet pup?"

He set Rudy free on the other side of the picket fence and returned to the truck bed for an armload of split firewood. Another pickup crept past, with Cash and Troy in front heading toward the stables, their speed kept to a minimum in deference to the layer of ice still coating the road.

Veronica knelt to adjust Rudy's sweater, then stroked him. "Thank you for bringing this cute little puppy with you. He's a lucky fellow to have landed with you when he raced out of the woods to disrupt that snowman contest."

Gil stacked the load on the porch so the guests wouldn't have to walk far to refill their fireplace. "Rudy is actually staying with Neve Dalton."

"Hmm..." Veronica winked, adjusting her ear muffs. "Looks to me like he's chosen you as his person. And I should know. I worked as a veterinary assistant for thirty years."

His heart pinched again at all the goodbyes ahead of him in a couple of weeks if he couldn't convince Neve to stick around. Gil walked backward, toward the truck, Rudy scampering alongside him. "He has plenty of people who adore him, that's for sure."

Veronica waved with both of her gloved hands. "Y'all have a good day now. Thanks again for dropping off all that firewood."

Jacob called as he opened the passenger door. "If you run out, just let us know. Although we hope to have the power restored before it's dark."

Veronica stood in between her two friends, hooking arms. "It's toasty warm in our cabin. Now, be sure you both give our best to your lovely ladies."

As another truck passed, this time with Hollie and the head landscaper delivering meals so guests didn't need to make the trek to the lodge, Gil settled behind the steering wheel. "You have quite a community here. Some days I can't get over what a tight-knit group you've cultivated. It's no wonder Isobel and

Zelda decided to stay and put down roots with their fiancés."

Jacob gathered Rudy closer and dusted ice from his sweater. "There's been a real serendipity in how the right people have come our way just as we were ready to expand. Such as how the local librarian and a temporary contractor became a couple, and he decided to stay. Much like when Doc Barnett fell for Eliza shortly after she became our stable manager. We're all a family, of sorts."

Family.

Gil couldn't deny the word packed a more powerful punch than ever, considering he was about to become a father. How long had he been chasing the ideal of family? Since he'd been orphaned? Since his adoptive mother died?

And now...since he needed Neve to help him give his son or daughter the sense of family he'd never had?

"Wish I could figure out how to convince Neve to stick around. Any advice?"

"On how to persuade a woman? Nope. Afraid not. But take heart and let Moonlight Ridge work its magic. If she's meant to stay, she will."

He'd already asked her about staying once before and it hadn't gone well at all. Why was it so hard for her to consider moving when her entire family was here? His too? It made sense. Unless there was another reason for rejecting him, something he had no hope of overcoming.

Gil swallowed hard, gripping the wheel. "You're

going to know soon enough, but I would want you to hear from me. Neve is expecting and the baby's mine."

Jacob's eyebrows rose in surprise, then he clapped Gil on the shoulder. "Congratulations. That's awesome."

"Whether she stays or not, I'm going to need some time off in May when the baby's born."

"Of course, whatever you need. Like I said earlier. We're a family. And family is always there for one another."

Jacob made it sound so simple. And after the night Gil had spent with Neve, he needed things to be that simple. He wanted her in his life. Not just for the baby.

Except he couldn't dodge the impending sense of doom he felt at Jacob's words about how if she was meant to stay, she would. Because in Gil's life, people left, no matter how hard he tried to hold on.

Sitting cross-legged on the sofa, Neve nibbled the pastry, finally able to eat even though she'd woken up three hours ago. Morning sickness was better lately, but not gone altogether.

She tried not to watch the window obsessively. Gil had said in his note that he would be back, and she had no reason not to believe him. Besides, he needed to return Rudy.

But she was running out of things to occupy her time here alone. She couldn't edit her work since her battery had run down. She'd finished reading her library book, a biography on Jane Goodall. She'd moved on to wrapping gifts until her hands ached. She was trying to rest and be careful with her health, but she felt...

Restless.

Furthermore, her festive air had crashed to a halt when she'd stumbled across Gran's old crystal ring, stored in a box full of presents. She and her sisters had been planning to give it to River Jack at Christmas, along with sharing Gran's final wish that the child she'd given up for adoption receive the promise ring from so long ago.

Today, the ring and Gran's wish hit home with her. Neve's hand went to her belly as she imagined how difficult it had been for her grandmother to give up her child. Neve already felt so protective of her baby. She couldn't fathom parting with her offspring. Let alone spending a lifetime not knowing where the child had landed or what sort of family had adopted the infant. But she understood her grandmother's reasons for doing so, for her son.

If only Gran could have known how well things turned out for her baby boy.

As for the child... How often must River Jack have wondered about his birth parents? For that matter, how often had Gil thought about his own birth family? She understood why he wanted to be present in their baby's life. And she was deeply grateful for that, even if she couldn't quite see how to navigate their future.

Her gaze gravitated right back to the window for signs of Gil and Rudy. Was this what co-parenting would feel like? Her sitting by a window, waiting for him to drive up with their child?

The thought made her queasy all over again. She tossed aside her raspberry pastry and reached for her tea instead.

What did their night together mean? More importantly, what if they each wanted something different?

His truck pulled into view, and her stomach gave a jolt. The happy kind. Not the queasy sort. So she pushed aside her worries and focused on the moment, on making the most of the butterflies before the world intruded.

She smoothed a hand over her long sweater and fleece-lined leggings. So far, the fire kept the place cozy warm, but she'd still put on her favorite fuzzy socks. Not the most romantic of outfits, but his ardor last night left her in no doubt of his attraction to her and she didn't want to risk catching a chill.

The door flung open and Rudy bounded in ahead of him. Within moments of Gil tugging off his coat, she stepped into his arms and kissed him, the familiar feel and taste of him filling her. His hands roved low and firm, lifting her against him.

A low growl of desire rumbled in his chest before he pulled back. "Good morning."

"Good afternoon, you mean," she answered smartly, drawing him into the living room where more of the pastries and fruit waited. She shooed Rudy away just before the little rascal absconded with a tart. "Thanks for leaving breakfast." She pulled the pup's winter gear off and made a mental note to buy a bigger size soon. He was growing fast. "How were the roads out there? Is everyone safe and warm?"

"The staff came out in force. Firewood and meals have been delivered. Anyone who preferred to come to the main lodge has been transported." He sat, tugging her down onto his lap, then reaching for a raspberry Danish. "Electricity should be on before dark."

"And your father?" She curled against the solid warmth of him. "I texted a little bit ago but haven't heard back."

"Priscilla just messaged me that he's napping. They still have power, thank goodness." He bit into the pastry, offering her a bite as well, but she shook her head. "I need to get some coffee. Do you want anything from the kitchen?"

"I'm fine, thanks." Savoring the sight of his broad shoulders and muscled chest filled her senses to the brim. "There's a pot already brewed and waiting for you."

He paused by the table full of wrapping paper and ribbons, his hand falling to rest on the small jewelry box. "What's that?"

Her mouth went dry at the wary look on his face. She wanted to snap back at him that he could rest assured she wasn't ring shopping. She stifled the words that would likely only lead to an argument, stealing this fragile bond they'd forged. "That's, uh, Gran's ring. It was given to her by River Jack's bio dad. My sisters and I decided to give him the ring at Christmas, along with a framed photo of Gran."

Pensively, he stared at the jewelry box for a moment before setting it back on the table and trekking into the kitchen. "Won't you and your sisters have trouble giving it up?" He opened a cabinet and withdrew a pottery mug bearing a Top Dog Dude Ranch logo. "I'm sure my father would understand if one of you decided to keep it."

"We would never disobey Gran," she said with a laugh, glad to be shifting back onto familiar ground and away from the awkward moment when he'd held that velvet box in his palm. "I still find it so interesting that this ring was made by River Jack's biological father, who he never met. And yet Jack ended up making jewelry out of crystals from the same cave."

"The whole nature/nurture dichotomy, I guess." Gil returned from the kitchen with a steaming mug of java in his hand. "I like to think I take after River Jack. I never met my biological dad. He bailed on us before I was born."

Wanting to ease the furrows trenching into his brow, she wriggled her fingers for him to sit by her again. "Did your mother tell you anything about him?"

"His name is on my birth certificate, but I have no interest in meeting him." He blew into the mug before taking a long swallow. "He knows who I am, and he never made any effort to find me. He sure never made an effort to help during those years my bio mom struggled."

She could hear the pain in his voice and thought of his insistence on being a stand-up dad—and yes, of being there for her as well. She rested a gentle hand on his elbow. "I hate that life had to be so difficult for her, but please know my situation is different from hers. I have a good-paying job and a supportive family. You're planning to be involved. This baby won't have the heartache you did when your mom lost custody."

"This isn't about me." He turned away to set his mug down, no doubt a move to shield his face from her.

To put distance between them.

In that way, at least, they weren't all that different. She found it difficult to share the vulnerable parts of herself too. But she really did want to find a way to bridge the gaps between them, to deepen their connection beyond the physical.

"Isn't it?" She rubbed a hand along his back until he faced her again. "I see the way you watch my every move as if I'm frail. But I'm stronger than you think."

She believed that, yes. Yet as she stared at him, waiting for him to respond, she realized how much she wanted him to see strength in her too.

A sigh shuddered through him, those worried furrows creasing his forehead again. "I do know that, Neve. I care about you, and not just because of the baby. You know that you've drawn me from the first time I saw you."

Her heart melted more than a little, especially while still so tender over the image of him as a boy wondering about his absent father and losing his mother. Tears stinging her eyes, she decided to take his words at face value for now, rather than risk ruining this pocket of time they had together.

Or maybe, she simply needed to take her time deepening their connection. It had to grow at its own pace so that the bond was strong. Stable. She could only offer so many pieces of her heart at one time, after all.

So for now, she would gladly sink back into that certainty of their attraction. Both for the pleasure of it and to allow them both time to come to terms with the shifting tides around their fledgling relationship.

She slid her arms around his neck again, tucking away worries about the future.

Chapter Thirteen

The next day, Gil parked his truck at the outdoor Christmas market in downtown Moonlight Ridge, Neve beside him with an ultrasound photo in her hands. The gut punch of seeing their baby on the monitor still had him reeling even an hour after they'd left their morning appointment with the obstetrician.

Protective urges filled him, for the baby and for Neve. Gil had brought a list of questions about lupus and pregnancy, compiled from his internet research the night before. That rabbit hole of data had him in a panic by morning. While the doctor had answered his questions patiently and in detail, there was no denying the facts.

High-risk pregnancy.

Ten percent chance of miscarriage.

Antibody syndromes, and increased risk of lupus flares.

Increased risk of diabetes and preeclampsia.

Having the physician end the appointment abruptly at the end, due to an emergency, had ramped the worries up higher than before. Gil suspected his anxiety wouldn't ease even a little until the baby had been safely delivered. He couldn't stop himself from obsessively checking for the telltale butterfly rash indicating a lupus flare.

His hands clenched around the steering wheel. The thought of her hundreds of miles away in North Carolina only increased the sense of dread. And he wouldn't be able to attend each doctor appointment for updates. Would Neve be forthcoming if a problem arose? Or would she downplay the concern? Already she bristled at the least indication of protectiveness.

He willed his heartbeat to steady before he said something that wrecked what time they had left together. The last thing he wanted was to increase her stress level. She'd requested an afternoon shopping at the outdoor Christmas market, and he intended to deliver.

"Which stall would you like to start with?" He tugged on his gloves. "I'm at your disposal for the rest of the afternoon."

She wrapped her scarf around her neck. "There's nothing in particular that I need. I just want to browse for the fun of it."

"Then, let's browse." He would turn himself into the best browser, for her, even though every part of him needed the outlet of snowboarding or ice hockey.

Stalls lined the street, filled with holiday crafts. Each with a specialty. Quilted stockings. Hand-carved Saint Nicks. Pine cone wreaths. Even a holiday door decoration made of old ice skates, yarn pompoms, and greenery.

And so very many ornaments.

Music filled the air, Old English tunes played on a recorder. The scent of gingerbread and cider wafted from a food truck.

Angling past a crowd watching Bavarian dancers, Gil kept a careful hand on Neve's back while she shopped, checking out nutcrackers, then snow globes, pausing by a display of ceramic ornaments, the personalized family sort.

Neve skimmed her fingers over a Baby's First Christmas one, shaped like a cradle with a little face peeking from under the covers. "My sisters and I were talking about names the other day."

"What's on the list?" He hadn't gotten that far, but then the past few weeks had been hectic, to say the least. Although he thrived when busy, a man of action.

Or at least, he'd always thought so before. But just now, when he considered the extra rounds of hikes he'd led the past few days, and the additional rafting sessions he'd taken on before his dad's surgery, he wondered if he gravitated to those things purposely during times of stress. Had he been using activities to avoid deeper issues?

"If it's a girl," she said wistfully, "I'd really like to name her after Gran. It's a rather old-fashioned name, but it means a lot to me. Do you have a problem with Alice? And we call her Allie?"

He tried to dial back in his thoughts after his unhappy self-realization. Naming their child was a big deal, and the conversation deserved his full focus.

"I think that's a great idea." Family was important to both of them. It was definitely a value they shared. "Perhaps my mother's name in the middle? Marie."

"Alice Marie Dalton." Her fingers traced along the cradle ornament as if inscribing. "I like it."

His smile went tight at being cut out of the name. "Alice Marie Hadley."

She rested a hand on his chest. "Or Alice Marie Dalton-Hadley."

Some of the tension eased away at her words.

"Perfect." He skimmed a kiss over her mouth to seal the decision.

She swayed against him for a moment before returning her attention to the table of crafts. Her fingers skipped along the display to a blue bootie. "And for a boy? Do you have a preference?"

Sticking with the family trend, he asked, "What about your father's name?"

Neve pulled her hand away from the bootie ornament. "We weren't all that close. Not like you and your dad. Is his real name River Jack?"

"Close," he said. "River John Hadley."

"Okay." She tapped her chin, pausing and staring into the distance before her eyes lit with inspiration. "How about a nod to Sulis Cave where your dad gets his crystals, the heart of the Moonlight Ridge legend. John Sulis Dalton-Hadley."

Her thoughtfulness touched him.

"That's inspired. And also a great nod to your grandmother's story that led you here." He brushed her stomach lightly, her coat belted loosely over the slight bump—a change over the past week that brought a lump to his throat. May wasn't that far away. "I was talking to Jacob the other day, when we were delivering firewood during the power outage. I told him I'll need time off when the baby's born."

Her shoulders tensed and she replaced the ornament in her hand. "I'll be in North Carolina. You realize that, right? May is a busy time around the ranch."

"I'm not indispensable." He tried to lighten the tone, too aware of how distance would make it all the more difficult to win her over. Because, yes, there was no denying he didn't want her to go. "Paternity leave is real for dads, too, these days."

He wanted to be a part of his child's life from day one, from changing diapers to singing him or her to sleep. He wanted to be one of those fathers who wore a carrier pack to keep the baby close to the heartbeat.

Neve licked her lips nervously. "We can hash that out as the time draws closer."

Frustrated that there never seemed to be a right time for a frank discussion about the future, he wanted to make his position very clear.

"Just so that you understand, I won't be pushed aside. Fathers have legal rights."

Her whole body tensed at the mention of legalities and he realized he'd pushed too far. Especially if he hoped to win her over.

"Neve, I didn't mean—"

"It's okay. You're right. This is your child, and I'm glad for his or her sake that you want to be involved."

Her words didn't reassure him in the least, because North Carolina was still too far away and he was running out of time to persuade her to stay. Besides, he could hear the distance in her voice as she placated him in the wake of his declaration.

Perhaps the moment had come for a more proactive approach to winning her over so Neve, their baby, and yes, Rudy, would stay.

He reached for a Puppy's First Christmas ornament and passed it to the cashier. "We'll take this one. And personalize it as Rudy Dalton-Hadley."

Sneezing, Neve reached for another tissue from the box on the coffee table, her eyes watering. She'd pushed herself too hard the day before, but she'd wanted to check out the Christmas market since they were already in Moonlight Ridge. And now she was paying the price. Her hand gravitated to the slight swell of her stomach. She needed to be more careful, mindful of the little life depending on her.

She sneezed again, miserable, but there were limited medicinal options she could safely take. A cool-mist vaporizer on the end table pumped cleansing moisture into the air.

Cell phone in one hand, wadded Kleenex in the other, she finished her video call with Isobel. "Thanks for checking in on me, but truly, I'll be fine once this runs its course. Fingers crossed, I'll be cleared before Christmas Eve. I'm just sorry I can't help you with Lottie."

They couldn't risk Lottie catching anything with her post-surgical, compromised immune system.

Isobel chewed her bottom lip, looking harried and worried, her hair in a messy topknot. "You have helped, more than you know. And I know you will again, once you're on your feet. For now, focus on taking care of yourself."

"I'm being completely pampered, no worries. The Top Dog community has been out in wonderful force." The local librarian had dropped off books and magazines. Eliza, the stable manager, had come by to walk Rudy while Gil was at work. "And Gil has too. River Jack's doctor advised him to stay away from his dad until he's sure he didn't pick up the bug from me."

As much as she appreciated his tending, she felt guilty for taking away the older man's help. Gil had hired an additional nurse to take the night shift.

Isobel glanced over her shoulder. "Hey, Lottie's ringing the bell, so I need to hang up. Love you, sister. Take care."

The call disconnected. Neve nudged aside the lap quilt and padded toward the kitchen. The planked floor felt cold through her thick socks, and she couldn't seem to get warm, even in flannel sleep pants and a sweatshirt. Gil stood at the counter, putting together a lunch tray and looking far too sexy in low-slung jeans and a pullover sweater.

His restless feet danced along to a jazzy holiday tune playing on his phone. He was being such an attentive nurse, but he must be going stir crazy.

"Thank you for making lunch," she said, joining him by the counter. Just behind him, a refrigerator magnet anchored the ultrasound photo. "I'll probably take a nap afterwards, so please go on back to work."

"We can play it by ear," he answered with a smile. "I hope the French onion soup isn't too bland."

"That sounds—and smells—heavenly." Her mouth watered and her heart warmed at his thoughtfulness.

"As good as grilled PBJs?"

She laughed. "I'll let you know."

Gil opened the oven, grabbed a pot holder, and pulled out the pan with cheese toast for the soup. "I tried to think of something different. My mom would make chicken soup whenever we got sick. My dad hated that soup."

She switched on the kettle to make a fresh mug of tea. "What did he dislike about it?"

"He said it was too watery. He likes hearty stews." He ladled soup into a pottery bowl. "But when I was feeling bad, Mom's cooking was like a tonic. And she always knew my favorite flavor sports drink."

"What flavor was it?" She drizzled honey into her mug, enjoying the ease with which they navigated this simple task.

"Grape, of course." He added the toasted bread on top of the crockery. "What about favorites from your mom and dad?"

She scrunched her nose, then stifled a sneeze. "My parents were so devoted to each other and their work, there wasn't a lot of time left for us girls. Gran stepped into the void. We spent at least half of each year with her. I guess you could say she had shared custody of us."

Gil didn't laugh, just stared at her with eyes unusually somber as he arranged her food on a tray. "I'm glad she could be there for you."

Moments like these, she missed Gran even more than normal. "When I was sick, my gran used to make cheese toast, with the really good cheddar, not the sliced stuff. So this is perfect, even if you didn't know ahead of time." Her nose clogged from unshed tears as much as the sniffles. She busied herself with pouring hot water over the tea bag and honey. "And she kept those little bottles of Coke in her refrigerator. Just for us three girls."

He carried the tray into the living room, calling over his shoulder. "Ah, and remember those popsicles in a plastic sleeve?"

"They still make them." She cradled the mug in her hands as she followed.

"Just think of all the great things we'll get to rediscover as parents." He turned toward her with a smile that took her breath away.

That same grin had stopped her in her tracks from the first moment she'd seen him hefting canoes into the water for an outing. She'd been so drawn to his vitality. His energy and enthusiasm for life. Why was it that people were so attracted to their opposites?

She cleared her throat, then stifled a cough that had her setting down her mug before she sloshed the hot tea onto her hand. Catching her breath, she took her place on the sofa again, dragging the quilt over her legs. "Do you have a preference of a girl or a boy?"

"I just want a healthy baby." He pressed his hand to her forehead, frowning ever so slightly with worry. "The gender doesn't matter. I'll be sledding and boating and fishing with the kid, either way."

And he would. She knew that about him. No matter what gender—an Alice or John Sulis—Gil would bring that child along for adventures early on. He was a natural.

Which brought a chilling follow-up thought... "What about when you meet someone and have children with her?"

He went completely still, all the more pronounced since he was a man of constant motion. "What are you asking me?"

More of those tears clogged her nose. "I want to make sure this child will be equally loved."

Kneeling in front of her, he took her hands in his. "I could ask you the same question, about future relationships and more children."

More children. With someone else.

Or with him.

Jealousy swelled inside her until she couldn't form words. Her chest went tight with panic. She recognized that the emotion was contrary. She'd been clear on them not having a future, and she wanted happiness for him. Still...

Thinking about all the ways tomorrows could spin out without one another was too anxiety-inducing.

Gil squeezed her fingers and pressed a kiss to her forehead. "Enough talking. Best to rest your voice. If you're serious about that nap, I'll leave you to enjoy the lunch while I log in a few hours at work."

She sat frozen, her soup and tea cooling in front of her, barely registering the sound of Gil tugging on his coat and closing the front door after him. Was it just her imagination, or had he been only too glad to leave as soon as the conversation hit tricky waters?

At the click of the lock, she sagged back into the pile of throw pillows and wished, more than ever, that she could call Gran for some much-needed guidance.

The dude ranch was buzzing with activity, guests and staff making up for lost time after the ice storm. Gil certainly welcomed the chance to burn off excess energy along with pent-up worries for his father and Neve. He'd just returned his horse after leading a trail ride, which timed well for retrieving Rudy from the stable manager's office.

"Thanks, Eliza," Gil called out in the horse barn. "I appreciate you keeping an eye on Rudy this afternoon and getting the traveling vet to give him his next round of vaccines."

Peeking from inside a stall, Eliza waved. "No need

for thanks. He and Loki had a blast chasing each other around the pasture. Oh, and congratulations to you and Neve on the baby news. You won't be in short supply of offers to babysit around here."

Word was spreading fast. He just hoped those same good wishes weren't going to pressure Neve before he had a chance. "Thanks, I appreciate it."

The scent of hay and whinny of horses filled his senses on the way back out into the cold. Rudy trotted right alongside him, already growing accustomed to the sounds and smells of farm life, which would distract many regular house pets. Rudy didn't even flinch when Pippa the cat raced past, no doubt in pursuit of an unseen mouse.

Gil had been working on the pup's leash-walking for Neve, envisioning her taking the little fella along on her nature walks. The pup even knew a couple of cues—Sit and Down. He was an eager-to-please, happy-go-lucky dog.

"Ready to go home, Rudy?" Funny how fast he'd come to think of the cottage with Neve as "home." He had his own cabin here at the ranch, but the place had never been more than a way station for sleep and changing clothes.

The Top Dog community was what made the place feel like home, not the four walls. Familiar faces everywhere. Hollie O'Brien closing up Bone Appetit, dog treats and ice cream shop, her Scottish terrier zipping back and forth on his leash. The tree farmer ice skating with his triplet boys on the rink with guests, blades *whisk whisking* in time with the music piping over the sound system. No doubt the boys' mother was still manning the gift shop.

An appreciation of simple pleasures radiated from each activity. This was the kind of life Gil wanted for his son or daughter, and not just for a few weeks a year.

Romancing Neve was proving to be a challenge, especially when he couldn't even take her out to dinner. So he would just have to get creative.

"Rudy, my boy," he said, adjusting the leash in his gloved hand, "let's make a quick detour."

A few steps off the beaten path took him by the greenhouse, where the head landscaper supplied him with all the best dried flowers and essential oils for sinus relief. Eucalyptus and peppermint. Along with a live Christmas cactus, pet friendly and sporting a fat red bow. He'd been schooled about the dangers of poinsettias to dogs when he'd initially asked for one. Not the best plant to have around a curious puppy.

By the time he finished the brisk walk, he'd burned off tension with each crunching step. The air was cold, but bracing, in the way that filled his lungs with the rural outdoors he loved. No city living for him.

The trio of sister cabins came into view and he spotted Lottie bundled up on her porch in her wheelchair, with Cocoa at her feet. Isobel stood at a far corner of the porch, deep in conversation on her cell phone.

Lottie waved. "Hey, Mr. Gil. Mama and me are

getting some fresh air for a few minutes, and your daddy's gonna drive by to wave to me, 'cause he's going stir crazy too. I think he's bringing *presents*."

"My father is driving himself over here?" He couldn't have heard right.

His dad wasn't allowed behind the wheel for at least six weeks. Gil bit back a curse. He never should have trusted his old man to keep himself stapled to that recliner.

Lottie giggled. "Nooooo. I meant to say that his nurse is driving him." She paused for a breath. "Whatcha got there?"

The energy in Lottie's voice, her return to excited chattering, all pointed to her improvement. Thank heaven. Although the doctors had cautioned his dad to be patient. To expect four to six weeks before energy levels returned to normal, and that it could take up to two months before returning to work.

Or to school, in Lottie's case.

He stopped at the picket fence, keeping his distance but so relieved to see the little girl so chipper. She definitely appeared to have more color in her cheeks than the last time he'd seen her. "Just a few get-well goodies for your aunt to help with her sniffles."

"I drew her a picture," Lottie said proudly. "My mommy put it in with some stuff that Aunt Zelda's baking. Tell Auntie Neve that I love her very much and to get well soon."

"Will do," he answered, sidestepping to keep from

tangling in Rudy's leash as the puppy pawed at the fence.

Zelda came bursting out of her cabin, her parka flapping open as she picked her way over, carrying a basket. "Neve really liked these scones the other day, which surprised me since she's never been particularly fond of them before. I guess it makes sense now. Cravings and all."

"I'm sure she'll enjoy them. I'll be snitching one for myself." He was running out of hands though. "Let me put Rudy in the fence and I'll come back for the basket."

"I'll just set them on the chair on your porch. Lottie's note is tucked inside." Her words tumbled on top of each other. "I don't want to risk catching her cold and not being able to help with Lottie. But I needed to do something for Neve. How's she feeling?"

"Better as the day gets going. Early morning was rough." Worry crept in again and he wondered if they should call the doctor again. He'd texted Neve a half hour ago but the message was still unread, so at least she was getting rest. "I've got a cool-mist humidifier running, and I've been making lots of hot tea with honey."

"But if her throat's sore," Zelda said, shivering as a gust of wind tugged at her open jacket, "maybe I should cook something else…"

"I can't speak for Neve." He didn't have that right, which brought him back to wondering again what rights he *would* have in the future. "But I *can* tell you that Hollie and Jacob are sending soup from the lodge for supper, along with homemade orange sherbet."

The Purl Girls had even tracked him down to give him a pair of booties Veronica had whipped up the night before, as thanks for the extra firewood. He'd tucked them in his coat pocket.

His first gift for the baby.

But if Neve returned to North Carolina as planned, then the booties would go with her. He would need to outfit a second nursery in his impersonal cabin that didn't qualify as a home.

Having said goodbye to his first home, losing one mom and then the other, he didn't take for granted the special sense of community here. Or the gift of having so much family nearby. And for some reason he'd yet to understand Neve simply didn't feel the same way.

As he headed toward Neve's cabin, he suspected he would need a lot more than a handful of eucalyptus and a cactus to persuade her otherwise.

Chapter Fourteen

River Jack kept the car window open a crack in spite of the cold, thankful to be breathing air away from home. Even if it meant being chauffeured around. He was ready to get back to living his life.

In fact, this surgery had been a renewal of sorts for him. He hadn't realized it, but he'd been deeply locked in grief over losing his wife. Yes, he still missed her. Not a day went by that he didn't think of her. But reaching out to help Lottie and her family had been good for him, reminding him how precious and fleeting the gift of life could be. Plus the surgery had brought him face-to-face with his own mortality. He'd realized he wanted to make the most of the rest of his days on earth. He was ready to start enjoying life.

Except first, he had to recover from donating a kidney, a more arduous process than he'd expected. He intended to do whatever necessary to get back on his feet as soon as possible. Which meant complying with his doctor—and his too-intriguing nurse.

Priscilla gripped the steering wheel, looking festive in a green plaid coat. Her silvery-blond hair was fluffy and loose around her shoulders. "Feel free to adjust the heater if you're not warm enough. And there's a blanket on the seat behind you in my winter emergency box."

A blanket on his knees? Was that how she saw him? The notion stung a little more than it should have.

Probably because from where he was sitting, she looked smoking hot. "I'm fine. Thanks though. I even refilled my water bottle before we left."

"Glad to hear it. Let me know if you get tired and we can head back right away."

Although driving this slowly, he couldn't imagine they would get anywhere fast. No doubt she was being careful not to jostle him as they navigated past the main lodge, aglow with Christmas lights. Snowmen still stood from the competition, only a little worse for the wear.

"Yes, ma'am," he said with a wink. "I know I could have waited until Christmas to deliver these gifts to Lottie, but I want her to see the pile of presents under the tree. That's part of the fun, wondering what's in each package. Shaking the box and guessing."

"Fair point."

"Given how she's spent a good part of the month recovering, she deserves to get every extra ounce out of the holiday wherever possible. I included a little something extra for her to open early."

She was a sweetheart of a girl, that was for sure. He'd been touched by the card she'd made him. Perhaps it was her disease that made her such an empathetic soul, or perhaps she was just wise beyond her years.

But she was still a child, and she'd been through so much.

"That's thoughtful. I'm sure she'll appreciate it." She turned onto the dirt road leading past the stables and toward the cabins. "What did you get for her?"

Thank goodness for online shopping. "A craft kit to make Christmas masks for a photo booth."

"That sounds adorable." Her smile lit up her face. "What a great way to make Christmas memories. Be sure to text me a picture." She tapped the brakes lightly to wait as a family pulled their sled across the road, heading toward the hill behind the barn.

"Of course, I will. And I'll make sure it's the silliest of the batch."

What would she be doing for the holidays? He'd just assumed that she would be with him on the twenty-fifth, although why should she since he would be with his son?

She'd said she didn't have children, but maybe she had other family? Why hadn't he asked? Because, yes, he wanted to know more about this intriguing woman.

He drew in a bracing breath as he prepared to ask a woman out for the first time since... Well, since he'd been dating his wife decades ago. "Once I've recovered, I'd like to take you to dinner."

Her eyes went wide with surprise. The car fishtailed ever so slightly on a patch of ice and she turned her attention back to the road, regaining control of the vehicle. "I'm sure our paths will cross at the lodge's dining hall."

He must have become rusty on dating protocol because he wasn't getting the message across. Time to go for a more direct approach. "I meant that I would like to take you out to a restaurant down in Moonlight Ridge."

"You don't owe me any thanks for my care."

Was she being deliberately obtuse in an attempt to let him down easy? Or was he not being clear enough?

His ego could take the hit of a rejection, so he decided to push ahead and take the risk. "I'm not talking about our patient-nurse relationship. I have enjoyed our time together. I thought you had as well. Maybe I read the signs wrong? With the painkillers and all. I would like to take you out on a date—once I've recovered."

She pulled the car off to the side of the road and placed it into Park, turning to face him. "You haven't misread that the attraction is reciprocal." She held up a hand before he could speak or reach for her. "But I'm not in a position to start a relationship."

That wasn't an outright rejection. There was hope to be found in her words. "Priscilla, I'm only asking you to have dinner. One dinner."

"Of course." She laughed self-consciously. "You're right. Now I feel foolish."

He shifted in his seat, careful not to wince and launch an avalanche of concern from his nurse that would only serve to sidetrack the discussion. "But for curiosity's sake, why are you off the dating market?"

Her gaze skittered away, down toward her hands, twisting in her lap. "You heard my nightmares. Between the PTSD and my brutal divorce, I'm far more comfortable on my own."

The pain in her words filled the cab. He couldn't deny the raw honesty in her voice and he had to respect her wishes. Even as he regretted not being able to convince her to give him a chance.

He also wanted to let her know the door was open. "It's dinner in Moonlight Ridge. Just think on it. I'm not going anywhere."

Her eyes flew up to meet his and she chewed her bottom lip for a moment before nodding. "You're a good guy. If this was a different time? Maybe. Suffice it to say, I'm on a dating hiatus." A forced smile tugged at her face before she shifted back in her seat toward the road. "Now, let's get those gifts delivered."

The rejection hit him harder than he would have expected, given he'd only asked her for a simple meal out. Although that refusal made him all the more determined to try again.

She put the car in Drive and navigated the final two turns to the trio of cabins where the sisters lived. The ranch wouldn't seem the same without the three Dalton ladies there. Zelda would be marrying Troy, moving in with him and Harper once their house by the training facility was complete. And of course Neve—and the baby—would be returning to North Carolina.

A movement caught his attention and he saw Lottie on the porch. Her mom was talking to Gil as Cocoa and Rudy took a quick run around the fenced yard.

River Jack pointed toward where Lottie waited and waved. "Perfect timing."

Priscilla parked in front of the picket fence. "If you don't mind, I'll just stay here and keep the car warm."

He started to mention how much everyone would enjoy seeing her, but then, perhaps that was the point of her decision to stay in the vehicle. She didn't want to get closer to people. She'd just told him she was better off alone.

"Okay," he acquiesced. "I won't be long."

Carefully, he eased from the car, bracing himself to avoid jarring his incision. His legs were a hint wobbly, his energy coming back slower than he'd expected, but he needed to push his endurance.

And his mental health couldn't stand much longer sitting in that recliner staring at the wall.

He opened the back door, the two bags full of gifts for Lottie and her family on the seat, and wondered how he would carry them up alone.

Swallowing his pride, he started to ask for help from Priscilla just as Gil came into view.

"Hey there, Dad," Gil called, pushing through the gate and closing it quickly before the dogs could escape. "Good to see you up and about."

"Feels even better to be out of the house. I was going stir crazy." He gripped the edge of the open door in what he hoped was a nonchalant fashion that wouldn't alert anyone to his flagging energy.

"We'll be hiking around in our snowshoes again before you know it, and your nurse will be on her way to her next patient."

The words drew River Jack's attention back to the woman behind the wheel of the idling SUV.

How ironic that just when he'd decided to live again, the woman he wanted wasn't interested. He didn't know a whole lot about Priscilla since she didn't like to talk much about herself. Although he understood her well enough to know without question, if he pushed her, she would bolt full tilt in the opposite direction.

Just when he was too short of energy to put up much of a chase. But perhaps a slow and steady, patient approach, opening up more about his life, might net results with Priscilla.

Plan set, he hauled his attention back to his son. "A snowshoe outing sounds mighty enticing son. Meanwhile, wanna unload these gifts for me?"

Two days into her cold bug, Neve woke up early from her nap feeling better, energized and ready to work. Hopefully, a good sign of a short-lived case of the sniffles. She didn't want to push herself, so instead of going for a walk in the woods with Gil and Rudy—as she would have preferred—she turned to work instead so as not to overtax her newly returned energy.

Instead of hiking in the cold, she would remain

at home. Proofreading. Answering emails. Making lists for her upcoming move back to North Carolina.

Squelching down the tightness in her chest at the thought of leaving.

Gil wasn't making her departure any easier, with being the most thoughtful fellow on earth. She'd been touched by how he'd brought her a Christmas cactus because flowers would die too soon and brought dried flowers with a scent to ease her sinuses. The smell of eucalyptus would forevermore stir thoughts of him.

She clicked through past emails and pulled up the address of the moving company that had transported her boxes to Moonlight Ridge—her research materials, computers, clothes, and all her favorite hiking gear. She clicked a link to their website, opened the start-service form and began to type in her information…

A knock at the front door stopped her halfway through typing her name.

She pushed away from the table, wondering who it could possibly be. Sidestepping a box full of crafting supplies from earlier, she made her way across the cabin. She swept back the curtain to peek, confused for a moment until she recognized the leader of the Purl Girls. She tugged open the door, letting in a gust of cold air.

"Hello, Veronica," Neve said, grabbing her jacket and stepping out onto the porch. "What brings you over this way?"

The woman looked sweet enough, but Neve wasn't inviting a stranger into her cabin. Even if that stranger was carrying a gift sack with a clear bag of cookies peeking out of the top and Neve's stomach was grumbling.

"I hope you don't mind my coming by," she said, looking too precious in her pink snowsuit. "I realize I'm not a part of the community. Not long-term anyway."

"It's been a delight getting to know you during the short time you've been here." Neve tugged up the hood on her parka, not particularly cold but being careful all the same. The sun was sinking and temperatures would drop fast.

"I wanted to check in on you and bring some treats." Veronica set the small brown gift bag on the rocker. "Your fella told me you've been feeling under the weather, when I gave him the booties I whipped up for your little one."

"Booties? How thoughtful. I'll be okay though. It's just seasonal sniffles. Thankfully." She hugged her jacket closer like a talisman. "I'm already feeling better after some rest."

"I'm glad to hear it." She tapped the present. "I hope you enjoy a little pampering."

"You already gave us those booties."

"That was for the baby. This is for *you*. You have to remember to take care of Mama," she said fondly, touching her necklace with four children charms, love and pride radiating. "It's nothing fancy. Just a little care package of throat lozenges, oatmeal-raisin cookies, and a crochet cover for your tissue box. I hope you don't think that's too old-fashioned."

Neve trailed her fingers along the Kleenex cover shaped like a rooster. Too cute. The gift made her feel a little guilty for keeping Veronica outside in the cold when the woman had been so thoughtful. Although Neve appreciated the fresh air, the sound of the wind rustling in the trees. "I love it. My grandmother had one just like it. Thank you. Everyone has been so generous. I've been wonderfully pampered."

"This place has been a gift to me and my friends." Veronica dusted off the other rocker and sat, making herself quite comfy. "We've known each other since high school, but life scattered us to different corners of the country. It's been too long since we had a retreat, what with COVID, then one crisis after another interfering. Now that we've had so much fun catching up and experienced the magic of the ranch for ourselves, we're determined to come here annually. I'll be sure to bring the baby a blanket when we come next year."

Next year? That felt forever away with so many decisions to make in the interim.

"That's sweet of you, but I don't live here." She thought of that moving form inside, just waiting to be filled. "My sisters and I just came for... Well, it's a long story. My sabbatical ends after the new year, so I'll be heading back to North Carolina. I'm a professor."

"Well, I'll just get that baby update from your sisters, then." Veronica paused before smiling knowingly. "I'm sure the ranch will miss that good-looking man of yours. His activities are quite popular with the guests—not just because he's so easy on the eyes. Is he here? I'd love to say hello and thank him for the snow-tubing adventure."

"He's not here right now. And, uh, Gil won't be moving to North Carolina." She fidgeted with the rooster tissue cover. "We're not a boyfriend-girlfriend couple."

She waited for the judgmental response. Would Gran have been disapproving? She hoped—believed—her grandmother would have been supportive, especially having had a complicated first pregnancy as well.

Veronica patted her arm. "It's better to figure these things out now, if possible, so you're not facing a break-up or divorce later."

Neve breathed a sigh of relief, hoping the rest of the world would be as receptive of her decision. "That's my thought."

Veronica's forehead furrowed. "I hope that you'll cut that poor boy loose before his heart gets broken, though, because he's obviously smitten."

The words blindsided Neve so fully she missed whatever else the woman said for a moment. Surely Veronica must have misread the situation, making assumptions that just weren't true. While Gil had been all-in with the child, he'd been clear from the start he was not interested in forever. The fear of commitment—of loss—radiated off him.

Veronica stood from the porch rocker. "Well, I should head on back to my cabin before it gets too dark. Hope you have a nice night with that not-boyfriend of yours."

Offering a tight smile in farewell, Neve gathered the bag off the rocker and returned to the warmth of the cabin and her mountain of paperwork. She needed to make the most of the quiet before Gil returned from his walk with Rudy. Hopefully, her nerves would ease by then, because the prospect of spending time alone together in cabin sounded…complicated.

She settled back at the table with her laptop computer, two cookies, and a fresh mug of hot tea, then began wading through her backlog of emails only to have a familiar address freeze her from the inside out.

The cookie turned to dust in her mouth as she clicked open the message from her ex.

Gil finished up his walk with Rudy just as the sun started to set, which gave him inspiration for his next plan to romance Neve. Dating options were slim, given her cold, but he enjoyed a challenge.

He charged up the steps, Rudy trotting alongside. The little guy was smart, picking up his leash skills and house manners with remarkable speed.

Opening the door, he called, "I'm home."

Home? The second the word fell out of his mouth, he missed a step, even though he thought he'd sorted through the whole homey-cabin vibe earlier.

Neve rose from the table, closing her laptop computer quickly. "I didn't expect you back so soon."

"We've been gone over an hour. Rudy's getting to be quite the power walker," he said proudly. "Since he's probably going to eat and sleep, I thought you might enjoy some time away from the cabin. If you're feeling up to it."

"Yes, please," she said, stacking folders and setting them on top of her laptop. "What did you have in mind? Not that it matters. I just need to get out."

Was it his imagination, or did she sound like a woman who'd had a rough day? He'd thought she was fine and in good spirits when he left to walk Rudy.

"Nothing fancy, but definitely in the holiday spirit. There are so many new Christmas lights since we were last out at night. We could pick up a to-go box from the lodge and check out the decorations."

"Perfect. I'll get my boots and coat." She paused by the table, her hand resting on a shopping bag with wrapped gifts. "If you don't mind, I made some secret-Santa gifts for the staff. I would like to drop them off."

He peeked inside but couldn't see past the tissue paper. "Do I get to know what's in here?"

"I made birdseed ornaments."

Shadows shifted through her blue eyes that he couldn't quite pinpoint. Something definitely seemed off. He waited for a heartbeat and when she didn't speak, he smoothed her ponytail over her shoulder.

"I hope there's one in there for me to hang outside my office window." He pressed a kiss to her mouth, lingering, wishing he knew how to chase away those clouds in her gaze. He eased back a step. "I'll settle Rudy in the bathroom with some food, water, and his bed while you get ready."

Would she notice how they'd already begun to fall into a family rhythm of sorts? He was trying his best to show her their relationship didn't have to be complicated.

Twenty minutes later, he was behind the wheel of his pickup, with a dozen gift bags delivered and two boxed dinners on the seat between them. The truck cab smelled of barbecue and fries, making his mouth water. "Could you pass over one of the sandwiches, please? The one without extra pickles."

Laughing, she opened the box with his dinner and nudged it closer before setting hers on her lap. "I can definitely tell I'm feeling better now. My appetite is back with a vengeance."

He bit off a corner as they drove past the barn, packed with townspeople trailing through the live nativity and petting zoo. The star over the manger glowed and carols filled the night air.

An archway of holiday lights illuminated the road out of the ranch property. "Looked like you had a busy day, judging by all the paperwork on the dining room table. Anything interesting?"

She nibbled at a fry with undue concentration, the green-and-red flashing glow from outside dotting the inside of the vehicle. "Just getting my ducks in a row before it's time to head back to North Carolina."

The reminder of her departure made his stomach drop. He bit back the urge to argue all the reasons she should stay, but didn't want to ruin the mood or risk pushing her away. Instead, he steered the truck toward the covered bridge with a large sign reading Please Visit Again.

A sentiment he echoed.

He forced his focus on this moment, on this date with Neve as they drove toward the valley, twinkling in the distance. "Looks like they've doubled the displays just this week."

She eyed him over the lid of her lemonade. "Are you sure a night spent viewing holiday lights isn't too tame for you?"

Was that a dig at him? He refused to take the bait. "It's a time-honored tradition in my family, and one I hope to share with our little nugget next year."

She looked away quickly and he decided now definitely wasn't the right time to question those shadows in her eyes. Something had happened while he was away this afternoon, something that had left her unsettled. While he didn't intend to pursue the matter now, he fully intended to revisit the subject later.

Because, no question, the time for him to solidify a relationship with Neve was running out.

Chapter Fifteen

Priscilla opened the SUV's back hatch and lifted the box from the ground into the vehicle. It was amazing how much she'd accumulated at River Jack's home in such a short time. Books. An extra coat. Warm fuzzy socks. And her travel Keurig, a necessity for longer work shifts.

Thumbing the key fob to close the hatch, she sagged back against a tree trunk. She should be happy her temporary job was finishing up early, before Christmas. He'd been cleared from needing extra help as long as he didn't start driving.

Her next wasn't due to begin until after the New Year, and the holidays stretched long and lonely before her.

Not because she'd turned down the date with River Jack, something she still could barely wrap her head around. She just hated…silence. The inactivity of a time when everyone else was with family. The quiet gave her too much time to think. Maybe she should find somewhere to volunteer, like a soup kitchen.

First though, she needed to say goodbye to River

Jack. Her handsome and charming—albeit semi-non-compliant—former patient, who she absolutely was not going to date. Resolve set, she turned toward the house, toward his studio where he'd ventured for the first time since his surgery.

She picked her way along the paver-stone path, heavily salted but still a treacherous trek given the slope. The temperature hovered right around the freezing point, the air bracing and pine scented from the woods nearby.

The walkout basement had been converted into an elaborate workspace, with bright lighting. Tools lined pegboards and one wall sported three different types of jeweler's saws.

Whitewashed floor-to-ceiling shelves were packed with clear bins, full of gems and wires. A drafting table was parked in a corner with sketch pads. A massive cork board held a number of his sketches. Rings, necklaces, brooches...

A few landscape images, as well as drawings of the people in his life. One of his son standing at the edge of a mountainside. Another of Lottie and Cocoa.

And River Jack.

Sitting on a high stool at a planked table, he sorted gemstones. He'd dropped weight during his recovery, in spite of her efforts with the Crock-Pot. But his color was good and muscle tone relaxed. No doubt she was using technical assessments to distract from the draw she felt to his broad shoulders and wiry frame.

She cleared her throat to announce her presence—

and stop herself from staring any longer. "There you are. I was wondering where you wandered off to."

"Well, hello there." He spun the swivel stool to face her. "I'm just working on a few last-minute ideas for Christmas gifts. I'll be driving on my own again before you know it."

Stepping deeper into the space, she trailed her fingers along a crystal-angel brooch. "Is that a hint that you're not going to follow the doctor's orders?"

"Don't worry. I'll be good." He eased to his feet, careful, but smoother than even a week ago. "My son would have kittens if I got behind the wheel too soon."

"He cares." Their father-son connection was heartwarming. While she was comfortable with the life she'd led, the holidays sometimes made her miss the connections that filled other people's lives.

"He worries, too much." He scrubbed a hand over his jaw. "His mother's death hit him hard. People assume just because he's a daredevil that he's fearless in matters of the heart. But that couldn't be any further from the truth."

"I wouldn't have guessed." The mention of his deceased wife caught her by surprise and she wondered at the timing of his comment. From the flash of grief across this face, she could tell the death hit him hard too. Was he even ready to date? "Gil appears to be all-in on wooing Neve."

River Jack shook his head. "Again, that's the outward appearance. Inside—" he tapped his chest "—he's still holding back. Much like he did as a child when he came to us. He did make progress, with time. Then my wife died, and Gil reverted right back to that outwardly bold, inwardly wary boy."

She understood well how trauma could make a person hold back the inner corners of themselves for self-preservation. Even at the expense of pushing away an offer from a perfectly charming man. A moment of doubt made her question herself.

He lifted the sorting bin from the table and walked toward the shelves. "But that's enough gloomy talk. What's on the agenda for you, after you finish your contract with me?"

"Nothing until after the New Year, but that could change. Doc Barnett knows I'm open to the work." She'd all but begged him to find her a patient.

He glanced over his shoulder, brow furrowed. "I hope I haven't left you in a lurch with my speedy recovery."

"I have my military retirement." She sifted her fingers through a bowl of lava beads. "I just do contract work to keep busy." To avoid the dreams that came with too much time on her hands.

"Well, I actually do have an ulterior motive for my question." He pivoted to face her.

Her hands clenched around the coarse little orbs. "What might that be?"

"I meant what I said about wanting to take you out to dinner." He held up a hand. "Nothing serious. I heard what you said about being on a dating hiatus. I owe you for all those great meals you cooked for me."

His request caught her off guard, scrambling her mind. She should have considered the possibility he would ask again. Certainly, she'd felt the chemistry zipping between them.

Her mouth went dry and she swallowed hard, finding it tougher to say no outright this time. "Would you mind if I think about it?"

A wide smile creased his face. "Consider it an open offer."

Neve stacked research books into a storage container, readying for her impending move home. She tried to focus on packing away the things that weren't Christmas related so she wouldn't disrupt the holiday vibe.

Although right now, she wasn't feeling particularly holly jolly.

The email from her ex hadn't helped. He'd reached out asking her to lunch upon her return, to ensure there were no tensions since they worked together. She'd assured him all was fine and in the past. No lunch needed. Any feelings she may have had for him were truly gone.

Sighing, she wedged an accordion folder full of paperwork into the last bit of space in the container before fitting the lid on top. She couldn't deny it any longer. No matter how much she enjoyed the safe haven of her home in North Carolina, she knew that Moonlight Ridge had found a place in her heart too.

She didn't want to leave the place or the people, but she had obligations. A contract at the university.

Even if somehow she could get out of her contract with her professional reputation intact, the person she'd sublet her apartment to was vacating her place come January. So with no one else living there meeting the mortgage payment, staying in Moonlight Ridge would be impossible—even if she could see her way clear to making such a monumental life change with no guarantees.

In North Carolina, she had a steady job and an affordable home. A stable life. She had to provide for her child.

A knock on the door echoed before Gil tucked his head inside. "Hello, beautiful. Are you busy?"

She shook off her doldrums and straightened. "Come on in."

As usual, he looked so handsome and rugged, his light brown hair ruffled by the wind and begging her fingers to smooth into place. He stepped deeper into the cabin, carrying a brown paper sack.

"I brought lunch so we can hang out for a bit before I go to a work meeting and the office party," he said, setting the bag on the table and greeting her with a quick kiss, the familiar kind of a couple. "Then I need to check on my father."

It amazed her how quickly they'd fallen into a routine together. But right now, with her world unsteady, she held her silence as he moved about her space, removing two boxed dinners from the bag and placing them on the counter.

"Dad says he's fine to stay on his own, now that his time with the nurse is done," Gil said, fishing into that bottomless bag for a container of soup, a cellophane bag of sugar cookies, and a water bottle, "but I'll feel better if I'm there overnight, especially since he still hasn't been cleared to drive. And of course, we'll have some family time at Christmas."

"Won't you have to work?" she asked, surprised to realize she hadn't asked him much about his holiday plans.

Then again, maybe she had feared getting too attached to him when parting was inevitable.

"I've got a full schedule on Christmas Eve with the children's festival. We'll be having everything from donkey rides to an outdoor scavenger hunt. We've even set up an escape-room game in a barn for the teens. Christmas Day, though, I have completely free and the staff that got Christmas Eve off will work."

"That's good." She hated feeling so awkward.

"Crazy to think that this time next year, we'll be getting our child photographed with Santa." He paused, tipping his head to the side. "Is something wrong?"

"No, nothing at all." She rushed to brush aside the concern that would lead to a conversation she didn't have the emotional bandwidth to explore. "I'm just packing up a few things to get ahead."

His smile faded. "I hope you're not pushing yourself. I can help if you just point me in the right direction."

Her gut insisted she tell him she had all under control, but she shouldn't be lifting the heavy box. "Maybe just move that container to the hall and stack it on the other one."

His jaw went tight, and he nodded. He hefted the container of books with ease, muscles bulging against the sleeves of his flannel shirt.

When he returned, he asked tersely, "Anything else?"

Frustration welled inside her, at him, at herself, at life that had to be so complicated. She'd achieved her goal in coming to Moonlight Ridge. They'd fulfilled Gran's wish to find her long-lost son. They were giving River Jack Gran's ring at Christmas. And most importantly, Lottie had found a kidney donor and surgery had been a success.

Neve's hand slid to her stomach protectively. "Gil, I've always been clear about returning to North Carolina. I've built a career there, and that's all the more important now that I have a child to support. I can't just quit without notice."

He took her hand and led her to the sofa, sitting beside her. "I get that you love your job, and hey, I realize you made a commitment for next semester." He squeezed her fingers, his eyes intense. "But what if you moved here after the baby's born? Just for the summer. We could give it a test run. I bet by the fall, you'll see how much easier your life would be if you just moved to Moonlight Ridge near all of your family."

With the warmth of him so close and the swirl of emotions making her world tilt, she wanted to believe things could be that simple. But how could she string him along—string herself along—like that and set them up for an even bigger heartache? "For one thing, moving is no small feat now, and that's before there's a baby to consider. I don't think that's fair to any of us, living in limbo for months on end."

His eyes closed, tightly, and he exhaled hard before looking at her again. "I don't understand why you're making this so difficult for us."

Her frustration and hesitancy shifted to irritation. "Difficult? Did you actually just call me *difficult*?" With her feelings already so jumbled and raw, that term was the final straw. "I know it's just a word… but…"

"I apologize for my word choice. But why can't we be together?" he asked, not denying her question. "We have amazing chemistry. We get along great. We share a child. And I care for you."

"Gil, I've told you before." She eased her hands from his. "We're too different. My illness will bring limitations to my energy—to my life—that will restrict what I can do. I'm not a risk-taker by nature, and this pregnancy curbs that even more. How soon before you grow bored?"

"Ah, Neve," he said, stroking the side of her face tenderly. "You could never bore me."

Her throat moved in a long swallow and she strengthened her resolve. "That's easy for you to say now. What if my health fails to the point I need a caretaker?"

"Then, it would be my honor to fill that role."

He made the vow with such sincerity her heart almost melted and tears stung her eyes. But she had to hold firm for his sake and the baby's.

"You say that now, but you can't possibly know all the ways that would affect your life. I've already had one breakup since my diagnosis." The email from earlier still stung, how someone could go back and forth with emotions, even at the expense of hurting others.

"He was a loser then." Compassion filled his voice. "And it's not fair that you put me in the same category."

She needed for him to understand. "It's *because* I want to be fair that I'm saying this. Beyond all the lifestyle differences, I also know you've been marked by losing your biological mom, then the mother who adopted you. I saw how you struggled during your father's surgery. Your heart isn't ready to risk the possibility of more loss."

"Neve…" His voice cracked with emotion. The pain filling his eyes was unmistakable.

And heartbreaking. "You say you want to take care of me? Well, consider this me taking care of you by saying we cannot have a future together as a couple."

A weary sigh wracked through him, the grief in his eyes shifting to a sad resignation. "You know what

I think? I believe this magical upbringing you keep talking about with your grandmother isn't the full story. I've been listening to your fond memories of the past, and it seems that each one starts with how your parents weren't around and your grandmother picked up the pieces."

The accusation cut her to the core. Except hadn't she just made judgments about his childhood? Could he be right, just as she was? If so, that proved a mountainous pile of baggage to overcome, far beyond just being different or worrying about her disease.

She cared about this man, no question. He was giving and honorable, exciting and sexy. And he deserved the simplicity of a smooth life full of joy and love. As did she.

Clasping his hands and resting her forehead against his, she gathered her words. "Gil, I believe this painful conversation has only made it clear to both of us. We are not meant for a future as a couple. We need to focus on creating a stable future for our child so this little one grows up free of the hurts that hold a person back." She gave his hands a final squeeze before standing. Her heart ached with the decision, but deep down, she knew that they weren't ready to be a couple. "I think it's best that you go now."

Gil twirled his fountain pen on the scarred oak conference table, trying not to look at his watch. He wasn't a fan of business meetings, especially ones followed by an obligatory office party. But he also recognized they were a necessary evil to his job. At least this position had far fewer than his previous employment.

At the moment, though, he needed to burn off energy after his argument with Neve. She'd sounded so final, with no hope of them building a future together.

He didn't have a clue how his conversation with her could have exploded so fast and with such awful consequences. He'd honestly thought he was offering a healthy compromise by suggesting they try life together during the summer. Yet she hadn't seen it that way at all. The more they'd talked, the further away she'd drifted, until the distance between them might as well have been miles. He'd failed Neve and he'd failed their child.

Dragging his attention back to the task at hand, he checked off items on the printed agenda. Other than the projection screen, the conference room carried a timeless air, with its log walls and massive stone fireplace. An antler chandelier overhead cast a warm glow over the gathered staff.

The goal of this meeting? Strategic planning for the next stage of expansion. Ranch owners Jacob and Hollie sat at opposite ends of the table, wearing their trademark matching-plaid shirts and jeans.

Hollie tapped the clicker in her hand, advancing to the next slide. "We're hoping to offer more retreats, focusing on wellness and using the animals for therapy. We've brought on a therapist for workshops in the past. But this year we'll have a full-time position opening to help us maximize our efforts."

Jacob interjected, "When we say 'retreats,' we don't mean the sort for corporate executives. We will be offering packages geared toward cancer patients and trauma survivors. We're in the early stages of talks with a nearby addiction clinic about how our program could provide a weekend package near the end of treatment."

Hollie nodded toward Troy. "We're partnering with Troy's rodeo-training center to start a rescue for abandoned and abused animals, where they can be rehabilitated. And, if possible, rehomed."

Jacob creaked back in his chair. "And we're especially pleased to announce that as of July, we'll be the home of a summer theater company. They will present a formalized production of *The Legend of Sulis Springs*, written by our local librarian and Isobel Dalton. Think in terms of *The Lost Colony* theater production located in Manteo, North Carolina. We want to keep the heart, the spirit, and the mystique of our community alive."

Hollie addressed her wish list of other potential projects for the head landscaper, the stable manager, and the gift shop manager before turning toward Gil. "And our last item on the agenda, we would like for you to put together a wilderness-survival proposal, an off-the-grid experience for guests."

Gil all but salivated at the suggestion that was right up his alley and an exciting opportunity to push the envelope. Then his insides stilled as he remembered

Neve's words about their differences. Was his approach to life exhausting for her, draining her limited reserves?

The notion made his chest go tight. He only half registered the rest of the meeting and the transition over to the smaller barn, where their office party was located. Live music filled the air and a buffet of fried chicken with all the fixings normally would have made his taste buds water. Except he could only think of how much he wished he and Neve could have celebrated here together, with their friends.

Hopelessness filled him, an unusual sensation, and he eyed the door, wondering how much longer until he could make a polite exit under the guise of taking care of his father.

He angled past one familiar employee after another only to stop short at the sight of Troy and Zelda, wearing matching Christmas sweaters. She waved before peeling away to speak with Hollie by the gift-exchange table.

Once Zelda was out of earshot, Troy clapped him on the back. "What's got you looking so down? I hope there's not a problem with your dad's recovery."

"Not at all." Gil pulled a tight smile for appearances, and to distract from talking about his messed-up love life. "He's regaining his strength faster than any of us could have predicted. He doesn't even need the nurse's help at home any longer. I'll still be bringing meals and staying overnight. Of course we'd already planned to spend the holiday together."

Troy frowned, scratching along his jaw. "Oh, I thought we would be seeing you and your father for Christmas dinner with the Dalton sisters."

Might as well cut to the heart of the matter. Everyone would hear soon enough. "My plans are up in the air right now. Neve and I aren't exactly on speaking terms." Which would effectively waste the few days he had left with her before she moved.

"I'm sorry to hear that." Troy set aside his beer bottle and focused his full attention on their conversation. "You two seem so well matched."

Gil measured his words, not wanting to misspeak to someone in her extended family. He settled on the simplest explanation. "Not according to her. She's convinced I'll grow bored with her quieter approach to life. I can't seem to convince her that we balance each other."

"Did you tell her that?"

Gil nodded, although he wondered if he could have made that point better. He'd never been great with words. "She's still determined to move back to North Carolina."

Troy quirked an eyebrow and reclaimed his longneck from the high-top table sporting a poinsettia. "Then, if you want to be with her, move to North Carolina."

The statement stunned him quiet for a moment. "My job's here. My father's here. Her whole family is here. Moonlight Ridge makes the most sense."

"But *she's* not going to be here," Troy responded

simply. "North Carolina has mountains and rivers and adventures, just like Tennessee. Look at how Jacob is even using experiences from there as models to incorporate here."

"Yeah, but..." That sounded too simplistic. "What about the family support we already have?"

He'd thought that she would enjoy being around her sisters. She had genuinely seemed happy at the ranch.

Troy shrugged, pinning him with a wise and serious look. "Bottom line, if you love her, then *she* is your family. Neve and the baby. Wherever they are— that's your home."

Why did it make so much sense when he said it, even though Gil had been turning the situation over and over in his mind for weeks. And yet...

Love?

Did he love her?

The answer flowed through him with a searing certainty. Of course he did. His world had shifted on its axis from the moment he'd first laid eyes on her. And brilliant woman that she was, there'd been truth in her words that those feelings scared him far more than skydiving without a parachute. She was 100 percent accurate there. The only thing that frightened him more at this moment?

Losing Neve forever.

Chapter Sixteen

Making gingerbread houses with her sisters and niece, Neve forced herself to smile and pretend the holiday spirit was alive and well in her heart.

But truth be told? Her heart was shattered, like a delicate ornament dropped onto the ground.

Her body was on autopilot, going through the motions of festivity. Her senses were dulled to the point she barely registered the pine scent from the live tree or the warmth of the crackling fire, plaid stockings hung in a line along the mantel.

Lottie rolled her chair closer to the table, reaching for the bowl of gumdrops to decorate her creation. "Auntie Neve, I'm so glad you got better enough to spend Christmas Eve with us."

Neve drizzled snowy-white frosting along her gingerbread home. "Of course. Girl time is the best."

The Christmas Eve celebration was simple since Troy and Cash were both working. Harper was working, too, with her dad. And as much as Neve enjoyed both of her sisters' romantic partners, she had to admit it probably made the evening a little easier for her, not having the men there tonight. Their presence would only underscore how alone she felt. She'd spent most of the previous night crying to the point she worried about making herself sick again.

Had she made a colossal mistake with Gil?

Today, she just wanted to crawl under the covers and pull the blanket over her head. But for Lottie, Neve went through the motions of celebrating. After everything the child had been through, she deserved an amazing Christmas with everyone she loved.

Across the table, Zelda filled tiny bags with oatmeal and glitter to set out for Santa's reindeer. "Troy should be done with his shift in time to take us on a sleigh ride to deliver the reindeer food."

Lottie pressed a few candy pieces into the globby frosting with precision while Cocoa slept on the ground beside her. The well-trained dog didn't so much as glance at the food, much less beg. "Will I still get to see the manger play? I promise to stay in the sleigh with my blanket so I don't get sick."

Isobel adjusted the bow on Lottie's braid, then smoothed a hand along her daughter's head. "That's the plan. I'm even bringing hot chocolate to warm us from the inside."

Lottie squealed before popping a gumdrop in her mouth mischievously. "Goodie! Cocoa and me can wear our matching scarves those knitting ladies made for us. They used the softest wool ever," she said, pointing toward the fireplace, "like on our Christmas stockings."

Isobel propped a gingerbread snowman against her house. "We'll go after you take your nap."

"Yes, ma'am." Lottie wheeled her chair back and turned toward the hall with Cocoa alongside. The dog's wagging tail lightly brushed the decorated tree, releasing a light shower of pine needles.

Following, Isobel called over her shoulder to her sisters, "I'll be right back."

Standing, Neve scooped up the wrapping paper and bow remains from their "girl time" book exchange, a tradition of theirs. Neve tucked the new baby-photo album and assorted board books into her canvas bag. She'd bought Isobel a journal, a romance novel for Zelda, and a coloring book for Lottie.

Zelda lined up cookies shaped like dogs in front of her gingerbread grooming salon. "About that sleigh ride, don't let us keep you from your Christmas Eve plans with Gil."

Her stomach knotted with a fresh swell of heartache. "He's working today."

"I meant this evening, after work," Zelda said, shaking tiny candy snowflakes along the roof. "I thought you two might be spending some time alone. Isobel did invite Gil and River Jack to join us on the twenty-fifth. I hope that's still okay."

"We haven't made plans." Neve looked down and away, staring to keep from blinking and risk releasing tears. "We had an argument, a really bad one." The sort that felt irreversible. "I don't know how we can ever repair the damage and go back to the way things were."

Zelda set aside the sprinkles, her whole attention on her sister. "Oh no, sweetie. Troy said Gil seemed down at the office party last night, but he wasn't forthcoming on details. What happened?"

Neve swiped her sleeve across her eyes and reclaimed her seat. "Gil is pressing me to make life-changing decisions faster than I'm comfortable with. He wants me to pull up roots and relocate to Moonlight Ridge. Permanently. I have job obligations and a career I've built."

Zelda patted her hand. "Of course you do."

Neve choked back a sob. "He said I'm shutting him out from fear of rejection, because our parents weren't around."

"Could that be a possibility?" Zelda asked tentatively, her face conciliatory.

Still, the words stung and Neve pulled back. "You're on his side?"

"I'm on your side." Zelda clasped her hand again, squeezing. "Always. You're my sister. I'm just asking questions *because* you are my primary concern."

Some of the starch left her shoulders and Neve gathered her words, hoping pouring out the pain would bring ease. But even thinking about the argument and their breakup amplified the ache. "Maybe some of what he said has merit. My last relationship ended because of my new health challenges. And while Gil is more understanding, a better man all around, I don't want people hovering because of my lupus diagnosis. I pride myself on my independence."

Zelda studied her for a moment before saying, "There's a difference between independence and isolation. I know that well enough from past experience."

Hearing Zelda echo a point so similar to Gil's gave Neve pause. Was she retreating into isolation? She preferred to think she was protecting her career and her choices, needing to feel like she had agency in her life. She hated to think that she was too stubborn to compromise.

Still, she struggled with the notion of living a life in limbo as he'd suggested. If things didn't work out between them after she made those concessions, moving again with a baby in tow, wouldn't the heartbreak be so much worse then?

Although she couldn't imagine a pain any worse than she felt at the moment. "What would you do?"

"I can't tell you what decision you should or shouldn't make. I'm just suggesting you be open to listening and compromise." Zelda leaned closer, pinning her with the intensity of her gaze. "Do you love him?"

Such a simple question. But one with earth-shattering implications. Could that explain the level of grief, of loss coursing through her? And she wondered why she hadn't allowed herself to consider it before now.

Allowed?

That single word brought home how tightly she'd been keeping her heart in check. It also made her realize how right Gil had been. She'd walled herself away from the possibility of committing her heart.

But now her feelings for him awakened in full force.

"Yes," she said softly, her voice shaking from the intensity of her emotions. "I love him."

Zelda smiled, hugging her hard. "Then, keep on trying to figure things out. You don't have to come up with the perfectly planned solution today. You two have the rest of your days to explore and grow and plan."

What had previously sounded like living their lives in limbo now felt like hope, all because she'd opened her heart to the idea of love. She felt like it poured through every inch of her, crystallizing her feelings and her thoughts, helping her to see a way forward. She didn't—and shouldn't—try to revert to the way things were. Things were different because of the newfound feelings filling her heart.

Hugging her sister right back, Neve couldn't deny she was exactly where she needed to be. With family who loved her, who understood her, who could help steady her when life turned upside down.

She just needed to find the right way to bridge the gulf she'd put between herself and Gil. A way to let him know that she wanted them to be a family.

Then inspiration struck as she thought of the marketplace they'd visited and how he'd been so taken by the personalized ornament. She had minimal time left and the gift shop would be packed, but with a little help, she could make her own.

"Zelda? Are you up to some impromptu crafting before the sleigh ride? I need to whip up some Christmas stockings."

Gil was ready for a Christmas miracle.

But if one wasn't forthcoming, then he intended to press on. He wasn't giving up on Neve and their future. Whatever it took, he was all-in. Although a sign to give him hope would sure help steer him in the right direction.

With his father in the truck beside him on his way to the dude ranch, Gil was reminded of holidays past, driving to see his grandparents. Except with his mother along, singing carols the whole way. Now his father hummed softly in the passenger seat, an echo tribute to those long-ago seasons.

He guided the pickup past the main lodge. A dozen people in Victorian costumes played handbells as families streamed in for dinner. Some guests preferred to dine in their cabins. Like Neve and her sisters.

With the memory of his mother's voice still whispering in his mind, he wondered what his mom would have thought of Neve. As fast as the thought entered his mind, the answer followed. His mother would have approved, enthusiastically.

And she would have been so very thrilled about her first grandchild. A lump formed in his throat.

At least he was able to spend the twenty-fifth with

Neve since he'd been working a full schedule the day before. The lights in her cabin had been off after the office party on the twenty-third, then again last night after he finished his shift. While he'd wanted to declare his love for her then and there, he was beginning to understand the wisdom of Neve's more measured approach to life. The past two days had given him time to think and plan.

His musings were cut short by the ding of text messages coming in on his father's phone.

Gil glanced over and found his father grinning ear to ear. "Dad? Anything important?"

"It's Priscilla," his father said with an excitement that went beyond a mere friendly exchange, "wishing me Merry Christmas."

"That's really nice," Gil answered simply as he followed the paw-print signs marking the roadways.

"And, uh—" his father grinned sheepishly "—she invited me to have supper with her tomorrow. Of course she'll have to drive."

Gil quirked an eyebrow, intrigued. His dad hadn't mentioned interest in a woman since his wife's death. "As in a *date* kind of dinner?"

"She uses the word *date*," he said with a laugh, his delight obvious. "I think that's a pretty good indicator."

"Well, congratulations, Dad. That's great." Gil wouldn't let the uncertainty in his own love life taint his father's much-deserved happiness. "I'm glad for you."

"It's nothing serious, but it's…" River Jack gripped the phone, his gaze still fixed on the screen.

"Something—someone—making you happy?"

His smile stretching wider, if possible, his dad nodded. "Yes, that."

Gil stopped the truck as a couple walked hand in hand across the street, tucking deeper in the woods. "Why not ask her to join us for supper at Isobel's tonight? I'm sure the Dalton sisters wouldn't mind since Priscilla was going to attend when we thought you would need her longer."

"That's a good idea. The worst she could do is say no." He grinned wryly. "She did once before, but this text gives me renewed hope."

Gil wouldn't mind a little of that hope for himself. But at least he'd learned determination from his father. It inspired Gil to know that his dad had patiently waited for Priscilla to decide there was something worth exploring between them.

The familiar trio of cabins came into view, nestled in the trees with a light dusting of snow on the ground. In front of Isobel's cabin, she stood bundled up. Cocoa and Zelda's little Maltese mix dashed to and fro while Lottie tossed a ball.

Gil shifted the truck into Park and grabbed the bags of gifts in back. As his boots hit the ground, the sound of handbells drifted on the wind.

Lottie waved to them both. "River Jack! Gil! Santa Claus came! He brought me a big dollhouse with lots of furniture and people. Mama says it's good for me to use my imagination. I can make up stories for my dolls. There's even a doggie doll that looks like Cocoa."

The little girl's excitement reminded him of what a true miracle this Christmas was, thanks to the successful transplant surgery. While Lottie still had a ways to go on her recovery, she radiated health and happiness.

"That's wonderful, kiddo." Gil lifted the bags in his hands. "I have presents for everyone, and something extraspecial for you."

Lottie tugged her knit cap lower on her ears. "River Jack already brought my presents over."

"Those were from my dad." He nodded toward his father, who was leaning against the front quarter panel, intent on his texting. Given River Jack's grin, things were going well. Smothering a chuckle, Gil turned his attention back to Lottie. "Some of these are from me to you."

Squealing, Lottie clapped her gloved hands. "Thank you, thank you, thank you."

"You're very welcome," he said, affection for the child filling him along with more of that hope for the future as he thought of family holidays shared with this child and his own.

Isobel crossed the fence, bundled up in a parka. "By the look of all you're carrying, you've outdone yourself."

"We have much to celebrate," he said, hoping there would be even more. "If you wouldn't mind taking these, I would like to have a word with Neve before I walk her over. I'll do my best not to hold up dinner and presents."

After he passed her the bags—all but one special package—to Isobel, he strode toward Neve's, his boots crunching on ice and gravel.

A jingle sounded along the road an instant before Lottie shouted, "Santa Claus! It's Santa Claus!"

Gil glanced back over his shoulder just as Saint Nick drew closer, riding in a buckboard wagon pulled by two Belgian draft horses. Santa waved on his way past, making the rounds to each of the cabins. Hopefully that jolly fella had some Moonlight Ridge magic in his bag.

Neve adjusted the stockings on the mantel and hoped Gil would understand the message she was trying to convey.

A message that she wanted a future together.

She touched the freshly sewn stockings in the row, each one embroidered with a name.

Gil. Neve. Alice/John. Rudy.

Their little family, the one she hoped they could find a way to build together through compromise.

At the echo of Gil's footsteps on the front porch, she smoothed a hand down her loose sweater dress, bright red, adorned with a wreath pin made of painted puzzle pieces. She'd enjoyed special time with Lottie, helping the child make one for her mom and aunt. And they'd painted a horseshoe for each of the men.

Her mind filled with all the activities she wanted to do with her child, with Gil as well.

At his knock on the door, she took a bracing breath to tame the butterflies in her stomach and reached for the doorknob. She would be seeing him for the first time since she'd realized she loved him. For an instant, she cradled the knowledge close, taking strength from it, then opened the door.

The sight of him stirred those flutters all over again as he stood there, so good-looking in his red sweater with a plaid flannel jacket that it was all she could do not to haul him back into her bedroom. The wind stirred his hair and she surrendered to the urge to smooth a wayward lock.

He lifted the shiny green gift bag in his grip. "Would you mind if I come inside for a moment? I brought an extra present I would like for you to open away from the crowd."

"Yes," she agreed, relieved he'd made the first step. "I have something for you too."

She backed into the cabin, waiting for the moment he would notice the new stockings, but his eyes were laser focused on her. He clasped her hand, his still cold from the outside. Leading her to the sofa, he sat beside her and passed her the present. The nerves in his gaze touched her and made her long to reassure him.

She opened her mouth to speak and he pressed a finger to her lips.

"Open your gift," he said. "*Then* we'll talk."

Curious and excited all at once, she pulled the tissue paper from the bag to reveal…a family ornament, much like the one they'd seen at the market. A family of three with a dog, inscribed in just the same way she'd personalized the stockings. Even including Rudy. She clasped it to her chest, her heart swelling. She started to direct his attention to the fireplace, but again he stopped her.

"Neve, wherever you want to live, I'll make it work."

She'd hoped for a compromise, but she'd barely dared hope he would make such a complete turnaround. "But you love your job here, and being close to your father."

"A new location is a new adventure." His grin lit his face, almost chasing away the worry furrowing his brow. "My dad would be the first to understand the importance of being a good father, a present one. He'll support my decision. I'll bet he visits often too. He'll want to see his grandchild."

She looked at the ornament then back at him, still questioning that she'd heard correctly. "You would do all of that for *me*? Leave your home and follow me?"

"I would do that for *us*." He slid his hands to her face, gently. "Because I have fallen deeply and irrevocably in love with you."

His words took her breath away, her thoughts racing to catch up with her galloping heart. She went to speak, but it wasn't easy to say anything with her heart in her throat. Besides, Gil continued, his words sounding so certain.

"Neve, I'm crazy about you for so many reasons. Your brilliant mind challenges me. Your tender spirit balances me. And your big heart humbles me. If you don't feel the same, I'll wait as long as it takes. I want nothing more than to spend the rest of my life proving myself worthy of you."

Tears stung her eyes, the happy kind. She held up the ornament, then pointed toward the mantel, finding her voice. "You won't have to wait that long."

Confusion chased across his face before he shifted his attention toward the fireplace. Then wonder and wary hope lit his eyes.

She nodded, resting her palms over his hands. "It seems great minds think alike—with starting family traditions and with falling in love. Because I do love you, so very much."

A sigh of relief shook him and he rested his forehead against hers. "I can't believe you're not showing me the door. We can celebrate the holidays with a lighter heart and then start packing. Together."

"What about your job though?" She pressed the point again. "I understand that your career is every bit as important to you as mine is to me. It's a vital part of your wild and free spirit that made me fall in love with you."

"Don't worry," he said, his face determined yet at peace. "I've already talked to Jacob and he's reaching out to some contacts for me."

"You're that serious?" she asked, surprised that he'd already started the wheels in motion. He really did mean what he'd said. "What if I had turned you down?"

"Then I still would want to be closer to my child. But I also want you to know that I would have wanted to move to be near you, even without a baby."

And with those sweet words, he gave her a gift more precious than anything else they could have ever exchanged. He loved her for herself.

"Thank you," she said. "For hearing me and loving me enough to follow me. Because, yes, you are right that there is a part of me that carries the pain of that little girl whose parents left her behind time and again."

"Neve…"

This time she stopped him from speaking, but with a kiss rather than a finger to the lips. "Let's not tarnish this with sad talk. I have some plans of my own to propose."

"Oh really?" He kissed her back, deeper, with a sweep of his tongue against hers. He growled low in his throat and shifted her onto his lap.

Desire and love bubbling through her veins, she slid her arms around his neck. "What about this? I have contractual obligations at the college through the beginning of May. I've worked hard to build my career, and I also believe in keeping my word. But I'm willing to consider looking for jobs near Moonlight Ridge that start in the fall."

He squeezed his eyes closed tight and drew in a deep breath before he tucked her closer against his chest. "You don't have to do that for me."

"Like you said earlier, *I'm doing it for us.*" As soon as the words left her mouth, she felt a fresh flutter in her belly but this time it had more to do with the baby than with nerves.

The wonder of it couldn't have been better timed. It felt downright magical.

Arching back, she took Gil's hand and pressed his palm against her stomach. "Feel that? Our baby is turning somersaults in agreement."

His eyes went wide for a moment, his voice soft with surprise and wonder. "That's the best Christmas gift of all."

And as he swept her into his arms again, she could have sworn she heard the chiming of handbells giving their ringing endorsement.

Epilogue

Fourth of July

Neve loved summer evenings, but this one was all the sweeter thanks to her new baby, her handsome fiancé, and their recent return to Moonlight Ridge. For good this time.

Moonbeams streamed through the branches of towering hemlock trees, dappling the quilt where she sat with Gil, their daughter in a carrier pack strapped to his broad chest. The infant's dark hair peeked out of the lightweight knit cap, the evening breeze pleasantly cool. Allie leaned her head against her father, her snoozing breaths coming out in contented puffs.

The feeling of contentment echoed inside Neve as they waited for the outdoor theater production to begin—the launch of *The Legend of Sulis Springs*. While the ranch had put on versions for kids in the past, this was a full-scale show, with a cast of all ages, authentic costumes, sets, and lighting. An incredible undertaking, it was already receiving hype that had generated a packed crowd.

She'd attended the dress rehearsal the night before and it was positively magical. She could hear Gran's voice and storytelling in her mind, like a whisper through the trees assuring them she hadn't left. Like the doe in the story, Gran was still with them, guiding their path.

Resting her head against Gil's shoulder, Neve pressed a kiss to Allie's head. Love swelled inside her for her child. For her child's father as well.

Live music played while she waited with her family, as well as the rest of the audience. A banjo, fiddle, and mandolin. Other instruments were perched on stands behind the players, even a washboard, ready to be swapped out during the performance. For now, most of the attendees brought blankets to sit on while watching from the hillside, while others viewed from bench seats closer to the stage.

Neve twisted the engagement ring around on her finger. The stunning diamond was set in a twisted silver that resembled vines with tiny emeralds for leaves. Designed by River Jack, of course. She appreciated how the one-of-a-kind creation reflected her love of nature, so personal and right.

She could feel Gran smiling down from heaven.

Her sisters, both married now, were a wealth of help in preparing for her wedding, with the big day slated for the fall. According to Hollie, their bridal album should be a model for future guests planning a wedding in Moonlight Ridge.

Neve tipped her face to the sky, soaking in the sensation of the mountain breeze across her cheeks. "It feels good to be home."

"And it feels even better to have all those moving boxes unloaded," Gil said with a wry grin. Rudy snoozed on the quilt as they waited for the show to begin, tuckered out from moving week.

Luckily, Jacob had been true to his word in helping Gil find employment during his six months in North Carolina, even holding Gil's job open for him at the Top Dog Dude Ranch. While in North Carolina, Gil had opted for a part-time position as a rock-climbing instructor, keeping his schedule light to make sure Neve had all the help she needed to stay healthy. And he'd done so in a seamless way, while reminding her they were a partnership. He'd also pointed out how she was doing the tough part in carrying their baby. By the time Allie had been born, Neve knew without a question...

They were meant to move home to Moonlight Ridge.

Leaving her job has been easier than she'd expected, thanks to an offer to teach at a local college. The campus offered on-site childcare, and she'd felt all the more peace about the three of them returning to the Top Dog Dude Ranch, near her family.

Gil's family too.

River Jack reached for his water bottle on the ground between their quilts. "How's Papa Jack's little princess doing?" Pure adoration shone on his face. "Is she still sleeping?"

Gil patted along Allie's back proudly. "Yes, sir. She's a master napper."

Priscilla hooked an arm through River Jack's. "Just like her grandfather."

The final piece of their grandmother's wishes had been fulfilled today when River Jack had asked Priscilla to marry him, using the ring his birth father had given his birth mother so long ago. Priscilla and River Jack's courtship had been speedy, although they planned to wait for a Christmas wedding, one year since they'd met. Their love was apparent to all.

"Yoo-hoo," Zelda called out, rushing across the field with Troy and Harper, bringing a picnic basket and an extra blanket. "I was afraid we would miss curtain time."

Isobel patted the ground beside her and Cash, proud stage parents, complete with a bouquet of flowers ready to give Lottie after the performance since she had been cast in the production. "We saved a space for you."

Space. The key word these days.

With their combined families, making enough room for everyone proved to be a glorious challenge. Neve, Gil, and Allie had been settled in a different cabin, a larger one to accommodate their growing family. The trio of cottages would always hold a special place in her heart, but Zelda had moved to Troy's home by his training facility just outside the Top Dog Dude Ranch. Lottie, Isobel, and Cash still occupied their three-bedroom cabin and even spoke of filling that extra room with a baby sometime soon.

Still leaning on Gil's shoulder, Neve wrapped her arms around him—and their child too. "Love you. Both of you."

"Love you too," he said, his voice soft and deep. Gil rested his chin on her head. "Have I told you lately how very happy you make me?"

"Just this morning, as a matter of fact." She tipped her face up to his, her ruggedly handsome man. "Have I told *you* how much I love you and our life together?"

"Yes, ma'am, you sure did." He angled to drop a kiss on her nose. "About an hour ago when we unpacked the last of the boxes."

She stared into his warm brown eyes until the outdoor lights went down, signaling a start of the production. The surety of their love left no doubt. They were in for the adventure of a lifetime.

* * * * *

Get up to 4 Free Books!

We'll send you 2 free books from each series you try PLUS a free Mystery Gift.

FREE Value Over $25

Both the **Harlequin® Special Edition** and **Harlequin® Heartwarming™** series feature compelling novels filled with stories of love and strength where the bonds of friendship, family and community unite.

YES! Please send me 2 FREE novels from the Harlequin Special Edition or Harlequin Heartwarming series and my FREE Gift (gift is worth about $10 retail). After receiving them, if I don't wish to receive any more books, I can return the shipping statement marked "cancel." If I don't cancel, I will receive 6 brand-new Harlequin Special Edition books every month and be billed just $6.39 each in the U.S. or $7.19 each in Canada, or 4 brand-new Harlequin Heartwarming Larger-Print books every month and be billed just $7.19 each in the U.S. or $7.99 each in Canada, a savings of 20% off the cover price. It's quite a bargain! Shipping and handling is just 50¢ per book in the U.S. and $1.25 per book in Canada.* I understand that accepting the 2 free books and gift places me under no obligation to buy anything. I can always return a shipment and cancel at any time by calling the number below. The free books and gift are mine to keep no matter what I decide.

Choose one:
- ☐ **Harlequin Special Edition** (235/335 BPA G36Y)
- ☐ **Harlequin Heartwarming Larger-Print** (161/361 BPA G36Y)
- ☐ **Or Try Both!** (235/335 & 161/361 BPA G36Z)

Name (please print)

Address   Apt. #

City   State/Province   Zip/Postal Code

Email: Please check this box ☐ if you would like to receive newsletters and promotional emails from Harlequin Enterprises ULC and its affiliates. You can unsubscribe anytime.

> Mail to the **Harlequin Reader Service:**
> **IN U.S.A.:** P.O. Box 1341, Buffalo, NY 14240-8531
> **IN CANADA:** P.O. Box 603, Fort Erie, Ontario L2A 5X3

Want to explore our other series or interested in ebooks? Visit www.ReaderService.com or call 1-800-873-8635.

---

*Terms and prices subject to change without notice. Prices do not include sales taxes, which will be charged (if applicable) based on your state or country of residence. Canadian residents will be charged applicable taxes. Offer not valid in Quebec. This offer is limited to one order per household. Books received may not be as shown. Not valid for current subscribers to the Harlequin Special Edition or Harlequin Heartwarming series. All orders subject to approval. Credit or debit balances in a customer's account(s) may be offset by any other outstanding balance owed by or to the customer. Please allow 4 to 6 weeks for delivery. Offer available while quantities last.

Your Privacy—Your information is being collected by Harlequin Enterprises ULC, operating as Harlequin Reader Service. For a complete summary of the information we collect, how we use this information and to whom it is disclosed, please visit our privacy notice located at https://corporate.harlequin.com/privacy-notice. Notice to California Residents – Under California law, you have specific rights to control and access your data. For more information on these rights and how to exercise them, visit https://corporate.harlequin.com/california-privacy. For additional information for residents of other U.S. states that provide their residents with certain rights with respect to personal data, visit https://corporate.harlequin.com/other-state-residents-privacy-rights/.

HSEHW25